W9-BWJ-806

FEB 1 5 2012

Dial-a-Dragon

The only light came from a circular window about twice the size of Mendanbar's head.

"There it is," said the dwarf. "If you want to see something, ask; but I can't guarantee it'll work."

"Show me Kazul, the King of the Dragons," Cimorene commanded at once.

For a moment, nothing happened. Then Mendanbar felt a tentative swelling of magic around the window. "I think it needs a boost," he said, and reached for his sword.

"No, let me," said Cimorene. She thought for a minute, then raised her right hand and pointed at the window.

Power surged around the window, and the glass went milk-white. "What did you do?" Mendanbar said, impressed.

"It's a dragon spell," Cimorene told him, keeping her eyes fixed on the window. "It's easy to remember, and it's not hard to adapt it to do just about anything. I found it in Kazul's—look!"

The window glass had cleared. Through the circular pane, Mendanbar could see the inside of a large cave. A sphere of golden light, like a giant glowing soap-bubble, covered half the cave, and inside the glow was a dragon. She was easily four times as tall as Mendanbar, even without counting her wings. An angry-looking trickle of smoke leaked out of her mouth as she breathed. In front of the bubble stood two tall, bearded men in long robes, carrying staffs of polished wood.

"Wizards," Cimorene said angrily. "I knew it!"

*Searching
for
Dragons*

Searching
for
Dragons

THE ENCHANTED FOREST CHRONICLES
BOOK TWO

Patricia C. Wrede

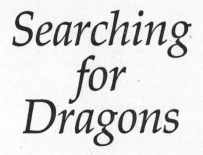

MAGIC CARPET BOOKS
HARCOURT, INC.
Orlando Austin New York San Diego Toronto London

www.HarcourtBooks.com

First published 1991
First Magic Carpet Books edition 2002

Magic Carpet Books is a trademark of Harcourt, Inc.,
registered in the United States of America and/or other jurisdictions.

The Library of Congress has cataloged the hardcover edition as follows:
Wrede, Patricia C., 1953–
Searching for dragons/Patricia C. Wrede.
p.   cm.—(The Enchanted forest chronicles; bk. 2)
Summary: With the aid of King Mendanbar, Princess Cimorene rescues the
dragon Kazul and saves the Enchanted Forest from a band of wicked wizards.
[1. Fairy tales.   2. Kings, queens, rulers, etc.—Fiction.   3. Princesses—Fiction.
4. Dragons—Fiction.   5. Wizards—Fiction.]
I. Title.   II. Series: Wrede, Patricia C., 1953–
Enchanted forest chronicles; bk. 2.
PZ8.W92Se   1991
[Fic]—dc20   91-8305
ISBN-13: 978-0-15-200898-7
ISBN-10: 0-15-200898-5
ISBN-13: 978-0-15-204565-4 pb
ISBN-10: 0-15-204565-1 pb

Text set in Palatino
Designed by Dalia Hartman
Printed in the United States of America
L N P Q O M

I would like to thank the

RIGHT HONORABLE WICKED STEPMOTHERS'

TRAVELING, DRINKING, AND DEBATING SOCIETY

—Caroline, Ellen, and Mimi—

for kindly granting their permission

for use of their Society

in this book, and for allowing me

to inflict them with a Men's Auxiliary.

Contents

*Searching
for
Dragons*

1

*In Which the King of the
Enchanted Forest Takes a Day Off*

*T*he King of the Enchanted Forest was twenty years old and lived in a rambling, scrambling, mixed-up castle somewhere near the center of his domain. He sometimes wished he could say that it was *exactly* at the center, but this was impossible because the edges and borders and even the geography of the Enchanted Forest tended to change frequently and without warning. When you are the ruler of a magical kingdom, however, you must expect some small inconveniences, and the King tried not to worry too much about the location of his castle.

The castle itself was an enormous building with a wide, square moat, six mismatched towers, four balconies, and far too many staircases. One of the previous

Kings of the Enchanted Forest had been very fond of sweeping up and down staircases in a long velvet robe and his best crown, so he had added stairs wherever he thought there was room. Some of the steps wound up one side of a tower and down the other without actually going anywhere, which caused no end of confusion among visitors.

The inside of the castle was worse than the outside. There were corridors that looped and curled and twisted, rooms that led into other rooms, and even rooms that had been built inside of other rooms. There were secret passageways and sliding panels and trapdoors. There were several cellars, a basement, and *two* dungeons, one of which could only be reached from the sixth floor of the North-Northwest Tower.

"There is something backwards about climbing up six flights of stairs in order to get to a dungeon," the King of the Enchanted Forest said, not for the first time, to his steward.

The steward, a small, elderly elf named Willin, looked up from a handwritten list nearly as long as he was tall and scowled. "That is not the point, Your Majesty."

The two were in the castle study, going over the day's tasks. Willin stood in the center of the room, ignoring several chairs of assorted sizes, while the King sat behind a huge, much-battered oak desk, his long legs stretched out comfortably beneath it. He was not wearing a crown or even a circlet, his clothes were as plain as a gardener's, and his black hair was rumpled and needed trimming, but somehow he still managed to look like a king. Perhaps it was the thoughtful expression in his gray eyes.

Willin cleared his throat and went on, "As the center of Your Majesty's kingdom, this castle—"

"It's not at the center of the kingdom," the King said, irritated. "It's only close. And please just call me Mendanbar and save all that 'Your Majesty' nonsense for a formal occasion."

"We don't *have* formal occasions anymore," Willin complained. "Your Majesty has canceled all of them— the Annual Arboreal Party, the Banquet for Lost Princes, the Birthday Ball, the Celebration of Colors, the Christening Commemoration, the—"

"I know," Mendanbar interrupted. "And I'm sure you have them all written down neatly somewhere, so you don't have to recite them all. But we really didn't need so many dinners and audiences and things."

"And now we don't have any," Willin said, unmollified. "And all because you said formal occasions were stuffy."

"They *are* stuffy," King Mendanbar replied. "Stuffy and boring. And so is being 'Your Majestied' every third word, especially when there's only the two of us here. It sounds silly."

"In your father's day, everyone was required to show proper respect."

"Father was a stuffed shirt and you know it," Mendanbar said without bitterness. "If he hadn't drowned in the Lake of Weeping Dreamers three years ago, you'd be grumbling as much about him as you do about me."

Willin scowled reprovingly at the King. "Your father was an excellent King of the Enchanted Forest."

"I never said he wasn't. But no matter how good a king he was, you can't deny that he was a stuffed shirt, too."

"If I may return to the topic of discussion, Your Majesty?" the elf said stiffly.

The King rolled his eyes. "Can I stop you?"

"Your Majesty has only to dismiss me."

"Yes, and if I do you'll sulk for days. Oh, go on. What about the North-Northwest dungeon?"

"It has come to my attention that it is not properly equipped. When it was first built, by Your Majesty's great-great-great-great-grandfather, it was naturally stocked with appropriate equipment." Willin set his list of things to do on Mendanbar's desk. He drew a second scroll from inside his vest and began to read. "Two leather whips, one Iron Maiden, four sets of thumb-screws—"

"I'll take your word for it, Willin," the King said hastily. When Willin got going, he could read lists for hours on end. "What's the point?"

"Most of these items are still in the dungeon," Willin said, rerolling the scroll and stowing it inside his vest once more, "but the rack was removed in your great-great-grandfather's time and has never been replaced."

"Really?" King Mendanbar said, interested in spite of himself. "Why did he take it out?"

The little steward coughed. "I believe your great-great-grandmother wanted it to dry tablecloths on."

"Tablecloths?" Mendanbar looked out the window at the North-Northwest Tower and shook his head. "She made someone haul a rack up eight flights of stairs and down six more, just to dry tablecloths?"

"A very determined woman, your great-great-grandmother," Willin said. "In any case, the dungeon is in need of a new rack."

"And it can stay that way," said Mendanbar. "Why should we get another rack? We've never used the one we have." He hesitated, frowning. "At least, I don't think we've ever used it. Have we?"

"That is not the point, Your Majesty," Willin answered in a huffy tone, from which the King concluded that they hadn't. "It is my duty to see that the castle is suitably furnished, from the topmost tower to the deepest dungeon. And the dungeon—"

"—needs a new rack," the King finished. "I'll think about it. What else?"

The elf consulted his list. "The nightshades are becoming a problem in the northeast."

"Nightshades are always a problem. Is that all?"

"Ah . . ." Willin cleared his throat, then cleared it again. "There is the matter of Your Majesty's marriage."

"What marriage?" Mendanbar asked, alarmed.

"Your Majesty's marriage to a lady of suitable parentage," Willin said firmly. He pulled another scroll from inside his vest. "I have here a list of possible choices, which I have compiled after a thorough survey of the lands surrounding the Enchanted Forest."

"You made a survey? Willin, you haven't been

talking to that dreadful woman with all the daughters, have you? Because if you have I'll . . . I'll use *you* to test out that new rack you want so badly."

"Queen Alexandra is an estimable lady," Willin said severely. "And her daughters are among the loveliest and most accomplished princesses in the world. I have not, of course, talked to the Queen about the possibility, but any one of her daughters would make a suitable bride for Your Majesty." He tapped the scroll meaningfully.

"*Suitable?* Willin, all twelve of them put together don't have enough common sense to fill a teaspoon! And neither have you, if you think I'm going to marry one of them."

Willin sighed. "I did hope Your Majesty would at least consider the idea."

"Then you weren't thinking straight," the King said firmly. "After all the trouble I've had . . ."

"Perhaps Your Majesty's experiences have given you a biased view of the matter."

"Biased or not, I'm not going to marry anyone any time soon. Particularly not an empty-headed princess, and *especially* not one of Queen Alexandra's daughters. So you can stop bringing it up every day. Do you understand?"

"Yes, Your Majesty. But—"

"But nothing. If that's everything, you may go. And take that list of princesses with you!"

"Yes, Your Majesty." With a final, fierce scowl, Willin bowed and left the room, every inch of his two-foot height reeking of disapproval.

Mendanbar sighed and dropped his head into his

hands, digging his fingers into his thick, dark hair. Willin meant well, but why did he have to bring the subject up *now*, just when it looked as if things were going to calm down for a little while? The feud between the elf clans had finally been settled (more or less to everyone's satisfaction), the most recent batch of enchanted princes had been sent packing with a variety of improbable remedies, and the giants to the north weren't due to raid anyone for another couple of months at least. Mendanbar had been looking forward to a quiet week or two, but if Willin was going to start nagging him about marriage, there was little chance of that.

"I might just as well go on a quest or hire some dwarves to put in another staircase for all the peace I'm likely to get around here," Mendanbar said aloud. "When Willin gets hold of an idea, he never lets go of it."

"He's right, you know," said a deep, raspy voice from somewhere near the ceiling. The King looked up, and the carved wooden gargoyle in the corner grinned at him. "You *should* get married," it said.

"Don't *you* start," Mendanbar said.

"Try and stop me," snarled the gargoyle. "My opinion is as good as anyone else's."

"Or as bad," the King muttered.

"I heard that!" The gargoyle squinted downward. "No thanks to you, I might add. Do you know how long it's been since anyone cleaned this corner? I've got dust in my ears, and I expect something slimy to start growing on my claws any minute now."

"Complain to one of the maids," Mendanbar said,

irritated. "We weren't talking about hiring a house-keeper."

"Why not? What are you, cheap or something?"

"No, and I wouldn't discuss it with you even if I were."

"King Mendanbar the Cheapskate, that's what they'll call you," the gargoyle said with relish. "What do you think of that?"

"I think I won't talk to you at all," said Mendanbar, who knew from experience that the gargoyle only got more unpleasant the longer it talked. "I'm leaving."

"Wait a minute! I haven't even gotten started yet."

"If Willin asks, tell him I've gone for a walk," Mendanbar said. As he left the room, he waved, twitching two of the invisible threads of power that criss-crossed the Enchanted Forest. The gargoyle's angry screeching changed abruptly to surprise as a stream of soapy water squirted out of the empty air in front of it and hit it squarely in its carved mouth.

Mendanbar smiled as the door closed behind him, shutting out the gargoyle's splutters. "He won't complain about dust again for a while, anyway," Mendanbar said aloud. As he walked down the hall, his smile grew. It had been a long time since he had taken a day off. If Willin wanted to grumble about it, he could go ahead and grumble. The King had earned a holiday, and he was going to have one.

Getting outside without being caught was easy, even without using any invisibility spells (which Mendanbar considered cheating). Willin was the only one who might have objected, and he was at the other end of the castle somewhere. Mendanbar sneaked past two maids and the footman at the front door anyway, just for practice. He had a feeling he might want to do a lot of sneaking in the near future, especially if Willin was going to start fussing about Queen Alexandra's daughters again.

Once he had crossed the main bridge over the moat and reached the giant trees of the Enchanted Forest, he let himself relax a little, but not too much. The Enchanted Forest had its own peculiar rules, and even the King was not exempt from them. If he drank from the wrong stream and got turned into a rabbit, or accidentally stepped on a slowstone, he would have just as much trouble getting back to normal as anyone else. He still remembered how much bother it had been to get rid of the donkey's ears he'd gotten by eating the wrong salad when he was eight.

Of course, now that he was King of the Enchanted Forest he had certain privileges. Most of the creatures that lived in the forest would obey him, however reluctantly, and he could find his way in and out and around without even thinking about it. He could use the magic of the forest directly, too, which made him as powerful as any three wizards and a match for all but the very best enchanters.

"Magic makes things much simpler," Mendanbar said aloud. He looked around at the bright green moss that covered the ground, thick and springy as the finest carpet, and the huge trees that rose above it, and he smiled. Pleasant as it looked, without magic he wouldn't have wanted to wander around it alone.

Magic came naturally to the Kings of the Enchanted

9

Forest. It had to; you couldn't begin to do a good job of ruling such a magical kingdom unless you had a lot of magic of your own. The forest chose its own kings, and once it had chosen them, it gave them the ability to sense the magic permeating the forest and an instinct for using it. The kings all came from Mendanbar's family, for no one else could safely use the sword that did the choosing, but sometimes the crown went to a second son or a cousin instead of to the eldest son of the king. Mendanbar considered himself lucky to have followed his father onto the throne.

Uneasily, he glanced back toward the castle, then shook his head. "Even a king needs a day off once in a while," he told himself. "And it's not as if they need me for anything urgent." He turned his back and marched into the trees, determined to enjoy his holiday.

For a few minutes, he strolled aimlessly, enjoying the cool, dense shadows. Then he decided to visit the Green Glass Pool. He hadn't been there for a while, and it was one of his favorite places. He thought about using magic to move himself there in the blink of an eye, but decided against it.

"After all," he said, "I wanted a walk. And the pool isn't *that* far away." He set off briskly in the direction of the pool.

An hour later, he still hadn't reached it, and he was beginning to feel a little cross. The forest had shifted twice on him, each time moving the pool sideways or backward, so that not only was it farther away than it had been, it was in a different direction as well. It was almost as if the forest didn't want him to find the place. If he hadn't been the King of the Enchanted Forest, Mendanbar would never have known he was going the wrong way.

"This is very odd," Mendanbar said, frowning. "I'd better find out what's going on." Normally, the Enchanted Forest didn't play this sort of game with him. He checked to make sure his sword was loose in its sheath and easy to draw if he needed it. Then he lifted his hand and touched a strand of magic floating invisibly beside his shoulder.

All around him, the huge tree trunks blurred and faded into gray mist. The mist thickened into a woolly fog, then vanished with a suddenness that always surprised him no matter how many times he did the spell. Blinking, he shook his head and looked around.

He was standing right where he had wanted to be, on the rocky lip of the Green Glass Pool. The pool looked as it always did: flat and still as a mirror, and the same shade of green as the new leaves on a poplar.

"Oh!" said a soft, frightened voice from behind him. "Oh, who are you?"

Mendanbar jumped and almost fell into the pool. He recovered his balance quickly and turned, and his heart sank. Sitting on the ground at the foot of an enormous oak was a girl. She wore a thin silver circlet on her head, and the face below it was heart-shaped and very lovely. Her long, golden hair and sky blue dress stood out clearly against the oak's brown bark, like a picture made of jewels set in a dark-colored frame. That was probably exactly the effect she had intended, Mendanbar thought with a resigned sigh. Somehow princesses, even the ones with less wit than a turtle, always knew just how to appear to their best advantage.

"Who are you?" the princess asked again. She was examining Mendanbar with an expression of great interest, and she did not look frightened anymore. "And how did you come here, to this most solitary and forsaken place?"

"My name is Mendanbar, and I was out for a walk," Mendanbar replied. He sighed again and added, "Is there something I might do for you?"

The princess hesitated. "*Prince* Mendanbar?" she asked delicately.

"No," Mendanbar answered, puzzled.

"Lord Mendanbar, then? Or, belike, Sir Mendanbar?"

"I'm afraid not." He was beginning to catch on, and he hoped fervently that she wouldn't think of asking whether he was a king. It was a good thing he wasn't wearing his crown. Ambitious princesses were even worse than the usual variety, and he didn't want to deal with either one right now.

The princess's dainty eyebrows drew together for a moment while she considered his answer. Finally, her expression cleared. "Then you must be a virtuous woodcutter's son, whose deeds of valor and goodwill shall earn you lands and title in some glorious future," she said positively.

"A woodcutter? In the Enchanted Forest?" Mendanbar said, appalled. Didn't the girl have *any* sense? "No, thank you!"

"But how came you here to find me, if you are

neither prince nor knight nor deserving youth?" the princess asked in wide-eyed confusion.

"Oh . . . sometimes these things happen," Mendanbar said vaguely. "Were you expecting someone in particular?"

"Not exactly," said the princess. She studied him, frowning, as if she were trying to decide whether it would be all right to ask him for help even if he wasn't a prince or a lord or a virtuous woodcutter.

"How did *you* get here, by the way?" Mendanbar asked quickly. He hated to refuse princesses point-blank, because they cried and pouted and carried on, but they always asked him to do such silly things. Bring them a white rose from the Garden of the Moon, for instance, or kill a giant or a dragon in single combat. It would be better for both of them if he could distract this princess so that she never asked.

"Alas! It is a tale of great woe," the princess said. "Out of jealousy, my stepmother cast me from my father's castle while he was away at war. Since then I have wandered many days, lost and alone and friendless, until I knew not where I was."

She sounded as if she had rehearsed her entire speech, and what little sympathy Mendanbar had had for her vanished. She and her stepmother had probably talked the whole thing out, he decided, and come to the conclusion that the quickest and surest way for her to make a suitable marriage was to go adventuring. He was amazed that she'd actually gotten into the Enchanted Forest. Usually, the woods kept out the obviously selfish.

"At last I found myself in a great waste," the princess continued complacently. "Then I came near giving myself up for lost, for it was dry and terrible. But I saw this wood upon the farther side, and so I gathered my last strength to cross. Fortune was with me, and I achieved my goal. Fatigued with my efforts, I sat down beneath this tree to rest, and—"

"Wait a minute," Mendanbar said, frowning. "You crossed some sort of wasteland and arrived *here*? That can't be right. There aren't any wastelands bordering the Enchanted Forest."

"You insult me," the princess said with dignity. "How should I lie to such a one as you? But go and see for yourself, if you yet doubt my words." She waved one hand gracefully at the woods behind her.

"Thank you, I will," said Mendanbar. Still frowning, he walked rapidly past the princess in the direction she had indicated.

The princess's mouth fell open in surprise as he went by. Before she could collect herself to demand that he return and explain, Mendanbar was out of sight behind a tree.

2

*In Which Mendanbar
Discovers a Problem*

Mendanbar was still congratulating himself on his
escape when the trees ended abruptly. He stopped,
staring, and quit worrying about the princess entirely.

A piece of the Enchanted Forest as large as the
castle lawn was missing. No, not missing; here and
there, a few dead stumps poked up out of the dry,
bare ground. Something had destroyed a circular swath
of trees and moss, destroyed it so completely that only
stumps and a few flakes of ash remained.

The taste of dust on the wind brought Mendanbar
out of his daze. He hesitated, then took a step forward
into the area of devastation. As he passed from woods
to waste, he felt a sudden absence and stumbled in
shock. Where the unseen lines of power should have

been, humming with the magical energy that was the life of the Enchanted Forest, he sensed nothing. The magic was gone.

"No wonder that princess didn't have any trouble getting into the forest," Mendanbar said numbly. Without magic, this section of forest couldn't dodge away from her; all the princess had to do to get into the woods was cross it.

Seriously annoyed, Mendanbar kicked at the ground, dislodging more ashes. He bent to touch one of the stumps. The wood crumbled to dust where his hand met it. Coughing, he sat back and saw something glittering on the ground beside the next stump. He went over and picked it up. It was a thin, hard disk a little larger than his hand, and it was a bright, iridescent green.

"A dragon's scale? What is a dragon's scale doing *here?*"

There was no one near to answer his question. He inspected the scale with care, but it told him nothing more. Scowling at it, he shrugged and put it in his pocket. Then he began a methodical search of the dead area, hoping to find something that would reveal a little more.

Half an hour later, he had collected four more dragon scales in various shades of green and was feeling decidedly grim. He had thought he was on good terms with the dragons who lived to the east in the Mountains of Morning: he left them alone and they left him alone. Glancing around the burned space, he grimaced.

"This doesn't look much like 'leaving me alone,' "

he muttered angrily. "What do those dragons think they are doing?" He began to wish *he* had not left *them* quite so much alone for the past three years. Right now it would be useful to know something more about dragons than that they were all large and breathed fire.

Absently, Mendanbar pocketed the dragon scales and walked back to the edge of the burned-out circle. It was a relief to be under the trees where he could feel the magic of the forest again. Frowning, he paused to look back at the ashy clearing.

"I can't just leave it like this," he said to himself. "If that princess came this way, *anyone* might get into the Enchanted Forest just by walking across the barren space. But how do I put magic back into an area that's been sucked dry?"

Still frowning, he circled the edge of the clearing, nudging at the threads of magic that wound through the air. None of them would move any closer to the burned section, but on the far side he found the place where the normal country outside the forest touched the clearing. He paused. It wasn't a very wide gap.

"I wonder," he said softly. "If I could *move* it a little, just around the edge . . ."

Carefully, he reached out and gathered a handful of magic. It felt a lot like taking hold of a handful of thin cords, except that the cords were invisible, floating in the air, and made his palms tingle when he touched them. And, of course, each cord was actually a piece of solid magic that he could use to cast a spell if he wanted. In fact, he had to concentrate hard to *keep* from casting a spell or two with all that magic crammed together in his hands.

Pulling gently on the invisible threads, Mendanbar stepped slowly backward out of the Enchanted Forest. The brilliant green moss followed him, rippling under his feet. The trees of the forest wavered as if he were looking at them through a shimmer of hot air rising off sunbaked stone. He took another step, and another. The threads of magic felt warm and thin and slippery. He tightened his grip and took another step. The trees flickered madly, as if he were blinking very rapidly, and the moss swelled and twitched like the back of a horse trying to get rid of an unwanted rider. A drop of sweat ran down his forehead and hung on the tip of his nose. The magic in his hands felt hot and tightly stretched. He stepped back again.

With a sudden wrench, everything snapped into place. The trees stopped flickering and the moss smoothed and lay still. The forest closed up around the burned-out clearing, circling it completely and cutting it off from the outside world. Mendanbar gave a sigh of relief.

"It worked!" he cried triumphantly. A breeze brushed past him, carrying the sharp smell of ashes, and he sobered. He hadn't repaired the damage; he had only isolated it. "Well, at least it should keep people from wandering into the Enchanted Forest by accident," he reminded himself. "That's something."

One by one, Mendanbar let go of the threads of magic he had pulled across the gap. He felt them join the other unseen strands, merging back into the normal network of magic that crisscrossed the forest. When he had released the last thread, he wiped his hands on his shirt, then wiped the sweat off his face with his sleeve.

"Are you quite finished?" said a voice from a tree above his head.

Mendanbar looked up and saw a fat gray squirrel sitting on a branch, staring down at him with disapproval.

"I think so," Mendanbar said. "For the time being, anyway."

"For the time being?" the squirrel said indignantly. "What kind of an answer is that? Not useful, that's what I call it, not useful at all. Finding my way across this forest is hard enough when people don't make bits of it jump around, not to mention burning pieces of it and I don't know what else. I don't know what this place is coming to, really I don't."

"Were you here when the trees were burned?" Mendanbar asked. "Did you see what happened? Or who did it?"

"Well, of course not," said the squirrel. "If I had, I'd have given him, her, or it a piece of my mind, I can tell you. Really, it's too bad. I'm going to have to work out a whole new route to get home. And as for giving directions to lost princes, well, it's hopeless, that's what it is, just hopeless. I'll get blamed for it when they come out wrong, too, see if I don't. Word always gets around. 'Don't trust the squirrel,' they'll say, 'you always go wrong if you follow the squirrel's directions.' They never stop to think of the difficulties involved in a job like mine, oh, no. They don't stop to say thank-you, either, not them. Ask the squirrel and go running

19

off, that's what they do, and never so much as look back. No consideration, no gratitude. You'd think they'd been raised in a palace for all the manners they have."

"If they're princes, they probably *have* been raised in palaces," Mendanbar said. "Princes usually are."

"Well, no wonder none of them have any manners, then." The squirrel sniffed. "They ought to be sent to school in a forest, where people are polite. You don't see any of *my* children behaving like that, no, sir. *Please* and *thank you* and *yes, sir* and *no, ma'am*—that's how I brought them up, all twenty-three of them, and what's good enough for squirrels is good enough for princes, I say."

"I'm sure you're right," Mendanbar said. "Now, about the burned spot—"

"Wicked, that's what I call it," the squirrel interrupted. "But hooligans like that don't stop to think, do they? Well, if they did, they wouldn't go around setting things on fire and making a lot of trouble and inconvenience for people. Inconsiderate, every last one of them, and they'll be sorry for it one day, you just wait and see if they aren't."

"Hooligans?" Mendanbar blinked and began to feel more cheerful. Maybe he wasn't in trouble with the dragons after all. Maybe it had been a rogue who had burned out part of his forest. That would be bad, but at least he wouldn't have to figure out a way of dragon-proofing the whole kingdom. He frowned. "How am I going to find out for sure?" he wondered aloud.

"Ask Morwen," said the squirrel, flicking her tail.

"What?"

"I said, ask Morwen. Honestly, don't you big people know how to listen? You'd think none of you had ever talked to a squirrel before, the way most of you behave."

"I'm very sorry," Mendanbar said. "Who's Morwen?"

"That's better," the squirrel said, mollified. "Morwen's a witch. She lives over by the mountains—just head that way until you get to the stream, then follow it to the big oak tree with the purple leaves. Turn left and walk for ten minutes and you should come out in her backyard. That is," she added darkly, "you should if all this burning things up and moving things around hasn't tangled everything *too* badly."

"You think this witch had something to do with what happened?" Mendanbar waved at the ashy clearing a few feet away.

"I said no such thing! Morwen is a very respectable person, even if she does keep cats."

"Then I don't understand why you think I should talk to her."

"You asked for my advice, and I've given it," said the squirrel. "That's my job. I'm not supposed to *explain* it, too, for heaven's sake. If you want explanations, talk to a griffin."

"If I see one, I will," said Mendanbar. "Thank you for your advice."

"You're welcome," said the squirrel, sounding pleased. She flicked her tail twice and leaped to a higher branch. "Good-bye." In another moment she had disappeared behind the trunk of the tree.

"Good-bye," Mendanbar called after her. He

waited, but there was no further response. The squirrel had gone.

Slowly, Mendanbar started walking in the direction the squirrel had pointed. When someone in the Enchanted Forest gave you advice, you were usually best off following it, even if you were the King.

"*Especially* if you're the King," Mendanbar reminded himself. He wished he knew a little more about this Morwen person, though. He wasn't really surprised that he hadn't heard of her. So many witches lived in and around the Enchanted Forest that it was impossible for anyone to keep track of them all. Still, this one must be something special, or the squirrel wouldn't have sent the King of the Enchanted Forest to her.

What sort of witch was Morwen? "Respectable" didn't tell him a lot, especially coming from a squirrel. Morwen could be a white witch, but she could also be the sort of witch who lived in a house made of cookies in order to enchant passing children.

"She could even be a fire witch," he said to himself. "There are probably one or two of them who could be termed respectable." He thought about that for a moment. He'd never heard of any himself.

If Morwen had lived in the Enchanted Forest for a long time, she was probably a decent sort of witch, he decided at last. The nasty ones generally made trouble before they'd been around very long, and then someone would complain to the King.

"And nobody has complained about Morwen," he finished.

*　　*　　*

Mendanbar reached the stream and turned left. Maybe it *had* been a mistake to cancel all those boring formal festivals and dinners Willin liked so much, he mused. They would have given him a chance to meet some of the ordinary people who lived in the Enchanted Forest. Or rather, he amended, the people who didn't make trouble. "Ordinary" was not the right word for anyone who lived in the Enchanted Forest, not if they managed to stay alive and in more or less their proper shape.

His reflections were cut short by a loud roar. Glancing up, he saw a lion bounding toward him along the bank of the stream. It looked huge and fierce and not at all friendly. As it leaped for his throat, Mendanbar batted hastily at a nearby strand of magic. The lion sailed over Mendanbar's head and landed well behind him, looking surprised and embarrassed. It whirled and tried again, but this time Mendanbar was ready for it. With a quick twist and pull, he froze the lion in the middle of rearing on its hind legs and stepped back to study it.

The lion roared again, plainly frustrated as well as embarrassed and confused. Mendanbar frowned and twitched another invisible thread. Suddenly the roaring had words in it.

"Let me down!" the lion shouted. "This is entirely undignified. How dare you treat me like this?"

"I'm the King," said Mendanbar. "It's my job to keep this forest as safe as I reasonably can. And I don't much like being jumped at when I'm just walking along minding my own business."

"What?" The lion stopped roaring and peered at him nearsightedly. "Oh, bother. I'm exceedingly sorry,

Your Majesty. I didn't recognize you. You're not wearing your crown."

"That's not the point," said the King. "It shouldn't make any difference."

"On the contrary," the lion said earnestly. "I'm the guardian of the Pool of Gold, and I'm supposed to keep unauthorized people from dipping branches in it, or diving in and turning into statues—that sort of thing. But if you're the King of the Enchanted Forest, you're not an unauthorized person at all, and I've made a dreadful mistake. I do apologize."

"You should," said Mendanbar. He looked around and frowned. "Where is this Pool of Gold you're supposed to be guarding?"

"Just around the bend," the lion answered. He sounded uncomfortable and a little worried.

"Then what are you doing attacking people over here?" Mendanbar demanded. "I might have gone right by."

"You wouldn't have if you were a prince," the lion muttered. "They never go on by. I was only attempting to get ahead of things a little, that's all. I didn't mean anything by it."

"Yes, well, you should have thought it through," Mendanbar said in a stern tone. "Princes don't always travel alone, you know. Someone could distract you with a fight along here while a friend of his stole water or dipped branches or whatever he wanted. This far away from the pool, you wouldn't even notice."

"That never occurred to me," said the lion, much abashed. "I'm sorry."

"Stick to the pool from now on," Mendanbar told it. "And make sure that the people you jump at are really trying to get at the water, and not just wandering by."

"Yes, Your Majesty," said the lion. "Uh, would you mind letting me down now?"

Mendanbar nodded and untwisted the threads of magic that held the lion motionless. The lion dropped to all fours and shook itself, then bowed very low. "Thank you, Your Majesty," it said. "Is there anything I can do for you?"

"Does a witch named Morwen live somewhere around here?" Mendanbar asked.

"Sure," said the lion. "Her house is up over the hill where the blue catnip grows. It isn't far. I haven't ever been there myself, of course," it added hastily, "since I have to guard the Pool of Gold, you know. But sometimes one of her cats pays a call, and that's what they tell me."

"Thank you," Mendanbar said. "That's very helpful."

"You're welcome, Your Majesty," said the lion. "Any time. Is there anything else? Because if there isn't, I should really be getting back to the pool."

"That's all," Mendanbar said, and bid the lion a polite good-bye. He waited where he stood until the lion was well out of sight, then continued on. He was very thoughtful, and a little annoyed. His quiet walk was turning out to be more of a project than he had expected.

A short while later, he passed the oak the squirrel

had described, and a little farther on he found a hill covered with bright blue catnip. He paused, debating the wisdom of walking around the hill rather than through the thick growth.

"You never know what things like oddly colored catnip will do if you touch them," Mendanbar reminded himself. He looked at the knee-high carpet of blue leaves, then glanced at the deep shadows below the trees at the foot of the hill.

"On the other hand, one of the easiest ways of getting lost in the Enchanted Forest is to not follow directions exactly." He looked at the catnip again. He did not want to spend hours hunting for Morwen's house just to avoid some oddly colored plants. Cautiously, he poked at the invisible network of magic that hung over the hill. It seemed normal enough. With a shrug, he waded in.

Halfway to the top, he saw some of the stalks near the edge of the patch wobble, as if something small had run through it. The wobble kept pace with him until he reached the top of the hill, but though he tried to see what was causing it, he was unable to catch a glimpse of whatever was brushing by the plants.

The patch of catnip ended at the top of the hill. Mendanbar stopped to catch his breath and look around. The hill sloped gently down to a white picket fence that surrounded three sides of a garden. A large lilac bush was blooming on one side of the gate in the middle of the fence, and an even larger apple tree loaded with fist-sized green apples stood on the other side.

Mendanbar frowned. "Aren't lilacs and apple trees supposed to *bloom* at the same time? What is one doing with blossoms while the other is covered with fruit?" Then he laughed at himself. "Well, it *is* a witch's garden, after all." He supposed he shouldn't be surprised if things behaved strangely.

On the other side of the garden stood a solid little gray house with a red roof. Smoke was drifting out of the chimney, and lace curtains were blowing in and out the open windows on either side of the back door. Below the right-hand window was a window box overflowing with red and blue flowers. The stone step outside the door was cleaner than the floor inside Mendanbar's study, and he resolved to do something about *that* as soon as he got home. Sleeping on one corner of the step was a white cat, her fur gleaming in the sun.

Mendanbar walked down the hill to the gate. A small brass sign hung on the latch. It read: "Please keep the gate CLOSED. Salesmen enter at their own risk." Smiling, Mendanbar lifted the latch and pushed the gate open.

A loud yowl from just over his head made him jump back. He looked up and discovered a fat tabby cat perched in the branches of the apple tree, staring down at him with green eyes. An instant later, a long gray streak shot out from behind a nearby tree and through the open gate. It slowed as it neared the house, and Mendanbar saw that it was actually a lean gray cat with a ragged tail. The gray cat leaped to the doorstep and from there to the sill of the open window. The white cat on the step raised her head and made a complaining noise as the gray one vanished inside the house.

"So much for a surprise visit," Mendanbar said to the cat in the tree. The cat gave him a smug look and began washing its paws. Mendanbar stepped through the gate, closed it carefully, and started across the garden toward the house.

3

*In Which Mendanbar Receives
Some Advice from a Witch*

*B*efore Mendanbar was halfway across the garden, the door of the cottage swung open. Seven cats of various sizes and colors trotted out, tails high. They flowed over the stoop, collecting the sleepy white cat on their way, and lined themselves up in a neat row. Mendanbar stopped and looked down at them, blinking. They blinked back, all eight at once, as if they had been trained.

"Well?" said a voice.

Mendanbar looked up. A short woman in a loose black robe stood in the open doorway. Her hair was a pale ginger color, piled loosely on her head. Mendanbar supposed she must use magic to keep it up, for not one wisp was out of place. She wore a pair of glasses with gold rims and rectangular lenses, and she held a broom in one hand.

"You must be Morwen," Mendanbar said with more confidence than he felt, for she was quite pretty and, apart from the black robe and broom, not witchy-looking at all.

The woman nodded. Giving her a courteous half-bow, Mendanbar went on, "I'm Mendanbar, and I was advised to talk to you about—well, about a problem I've discovered. I hope you weren't on your way out." He indicated the broom.

Morwen examined him for another moment, then nodded briskly. "So *you're* the King. Come in and tell me why you're here, and I'll see what I can do for you."

"How do you know I'm the King?" Mendanbar asked as the cats exchanged glances and then began wandering off in various directions. He felt disgruntled, because he had not intended to mention the fact. At least Morwen wasn't curtsying or simpering, and she hadn't started calling him "Your Majesty" yet, either. Perhaps it would be all right.

"I recognize you, of course," Morwen said. She set the broom against the wall behind the door as she spoke. "You've let your hair get a bit long, but that doesn't make much difference, one way or another. And Mendanbar isn't exactly a common name these days. Are you going to stand there all day?"

"I'm sorry," Mendanbar said, following Morwen into the house. "I didn't realize we'd met before."

"We haven't," Morwen said. "When I moved to the Enchanted Forest five years ago, I made sure I knew what you looked like. I'd have been asking for trouble, otherwise."

"Oh," said Mendanbar, taken aback. He had never thought of himself as one of the hazards of the Enchanted Forest that someone might wish to be prepared for, and he did not like the idea much, now that it had been pointed out to him.

Morwen waved at a sturdy chair next to a large table in the center of the room. "Sit down. Would you like some cider?"

"That sounds very good." Mendanbar took the chair while Morwen crossed to a cupboard on the far wall and began taking mugs and bottles out of it. He was glad to have a minute to collect his wits. He was not sure what he had expected her to be like, but Morwen was definitely not it.

Her house was not what he had expected, either. The inside was as neat and clean as the outside. The walls of the single large room were painted a pale, silvery gray. Six large windows let in light and air from all directions. There were no gargoyles or grimacing faces or wild tangles of trees and vines carved into the window ledges or the woodwork around the ceiling, and no intricate patterns set into the floorboards. One of the cats had come inside and was sitting on a big, square trunk, washing his paws; another was lying in an open window, keeping an eye on the backyard. There was a large black stove in the corner by the cupboard, and three more chairs around the table where Mendanbar was sitting. It was all very pleasant and uncluttered, and Mendanbar found himself wishing he had a few rooms like this in his castle.

"There," said Morwen as she set a large blue jug and two matching mugs in the center of the table. "Now, tell me about this problem of yours."

Mendanbar cleared his throat and began. "About an hour ago, I ran across a section of the Enchanted Forest that had been destroyed. The trees had been burned to stumps and there wasn't even any moss left on the ground. I'm afraid it may have been a rogue dragon. I found dragon scales in the ashes, and a squirrel suggested I come and see you."

"Dragon scales?" Morwen pressed her lips together, looking very grim indeed. "Did you bring them with you?"

"Yes," said Mendanbar. He dug the scales out of his pocket and spread them out on the table.

"Hmmm," said Morwen, bending over the table. "I don't like the look of this."

"Can you tell anything about this dragon from his scales?" Mendanbar asked.

"For one thing, these scales aren't all from the same dragon," Morwen said. Her frown deepened. "At least, they shouldn't be."

"How can you tell?" Mendanbar asked, his stomach sinking.

"Look at the colors. This one is yellow-green; that one has a grayish tinge, and this one has a purple sheen. You don't get that kind of variation on one dragon."

"Oh, no," Mendanbar groaned, shutting his eyes and leaning his forehead against his hands. He had so hoped that it had been a single dragon. It would have been a nuisance, sending letters of complaint to the King of the Dragons and waiting for an answer, but it would have been better than a war. If a group of dragons had attacked the Enchanted Forest, war was almost inevitable. "You're *sure* there were several dragons involved?"

"I didn't say that," Morwen snapped. "I said that these scales look as if they came from different dragons."

"But if the scales came from different dragons—"

"I didn't say that, either," Morwen said. "I said they *looked* as if they came from different dragons. Have a little patience, Mendanbar."

Mendanbar opened his mouth to say something else, then closed it again. Morwen was staring with great concentration at one of the scales, the one that was the brightest green, and she didn't look as if she would welcome an interruption. Suddenly she straightened and in one swift movement scooped the scales together like a pile of cards. She tapped the stack against the tabletop to straighten it, then set it down with an air of satisfaction.

"Ha! I thought there was something odd about these," she said, half to herself.

"What is it?"

"Just a minute and I'll show you." Morwen went back to the cupboard and took down a small bowl and several jars of various sizes. As she spooned and mixed and muttered, Mendanbar felt magic gather around her, like a tingling in the air that slowly concentrated itself inside the bowl. At last she capped the jars and carried the bowl, brimming with magic, over to the table.

"Stay back," she warned when Mendanbar leaned forward to get a better view.

Mendanbar sat back, watching closely, as Morwen spread the five dragon scales out in a line. She set the purple scale at one end and the bright green one at the other. Then she held the bowl over the center of the line, took a deep breath, and said,

> "Wind for clarity,
> Stone for endurance,
> Stream for change,
> Fire for truth:
> Be what you are!"

As she spoke, she tilted the bowl and poured a continuous line of dark liquid in a long stripe across the middle of the five scales.

There was a flash of purple light, and the liquid began to glow. The glow spread outward, like fire creeping around the edges of a piece of paper, until it reached the rims of the dragon scales. Then it flashed once more and vanished.

Five identical scales lay side by side on the table, all of them bright green.

"I thought so," Morwen said with satisfaction. "These scales all came from the same dragon. Someone altered them so that they would each look different."

"Oh, good," Mendanbar said with some relief. "How did you know?"

"The scales were the same shape, and very nearly the same size," Morwen said. "Different dragons might have scales about the same size, if they were the same

34

age, but there's as much variation in the shape of dragon scales as there is in their color."

"Really?" Mendanbar said, interested. "I didn't know that."

"Not many people do. But look at these—they're all round, with one flat edge. If they'd come from different dragons, I'd expect one to be, say, squared off, another oval, another long and wiggly, and so on."

"In that case, it shouldn't be too hard to find the dragon who destroyed that chunk of forest," Mendanbar said.

Morwen looked at him severely over the tops of her spectacles. "I'm not sure it was a dragon at all."

"Why not?" Mendanbar asked. "Because the scales were changed? But if he didn't want to be blamed—"

"If some dragon wanted to avoid being blamed for burning up a piece of the Enchanted Forest, he wouldn't have left his scales lying around, changed or not," Morwen said dryly. "Picking them up would be a lot easier than enchanting them. Besides, a healthy dragon doesn't shed scales at this rate. Unless you think your rogue dragon burned down a lot of trees and then stood around looking at them for a week or two."

"I see." Mendanbar picked up one of the scales and ran his fingertips across it.

"It's a good thing you were the one who found these," Morwen went on, waving at the dragon scales. "If it had been one of the elves, there would have been trouble for certain."

"Why do you say that? Whoever found them would have had to bring them to the castle—"

"And long before he got there, word would have

35

been all over the forest that a lot of dragons had burned half the woods to powder," Morwen said. "Most elves mean well, but they can't keep a secret and they have no common sense to speak of. Flighty creatures."

"Do you think someone was trying to make trouble between the Enchanted Forest and the dragons, then?"

"It's possible," Morwen answered. "If you hadn't come to me, you probably would have thought the scales came from different dragons. Plenty of people know about the color variation. I doubt that you'd have figured out the transformation, though. Only people who are fairly familiar with dragons know about the differences in the shapes of their scales, and I don't think anyone at the castle understands dragons very well."

"How do you happen to know so much about dragons?" Mendanbar asked, nettled.

"Oh, Kazul and I have been friends for a long time," Morwen said. "We trade favors now and then. She lets me have a spare scale when I need one for a spell, and I lend her books from my library and pots and pans that she doesn't want to keep around all the time. In fact, Kazul was the one who convinced me that it would be a good idea to move to the Enchanted Forest."

"Kazul," Mendanbar said, frowning. "That name is familiar. Who is she?"

"Kazul is the King of the Dragons," Morwen said. "Drink your cider."

Automatically, Mendanbar lifted his mug. Then the implications of what Morwen had said sank in, and he choked. Morwen was a good friend of the King of the Dragons? No wonder she knew so much about dragon scales!

Morwen gave him an ironic look, as if she knew exactly what he was thinking. To give himself time to recover, Mendanbar sipped at his cider. It was cold and sweet and tangy, and it fizzed as it slid across his tongue. He looked at the mug in surprise and took a longer drink. It was just as tasty the second time. "This is very good."

Morwen looked almost smug. "I make it myself. You may have a bottle to take back to the castle with you, provided you take a bottle to Kazul when you go see her about these scales you found."

"Thank—wait a minute, what makes you think I'm going to see Kazul?"

"How else are you going to find out who these scales belong to? I may know more about dragons than most people, but I can't tell whose scales these are just from their color and size. Kazul can. Besides, you should have paid a call last year, when the old king died and Kazul got the crown."

"I sent a note and a coronation present," Mendanbar said. He sounded sulky even to himself, and he felt as if he were being lectured by his mother, who had died when he was fourteen. "I was going to visit, but the Frost Giants decided to come south early, and then some fool magician tried to turn a rock snake into a bird and got a cockatrice, and—"

"—and it's been one thing after another, and you've never found the time," Morwen said. "Really,

Mendanbar. Haven't you learned by now that it's *always* one thing after another? Being busy is no excuse. Everyone's busy. You take those scales and a bottle of my cider and go talk to Kazul. At the very least, you'll get some good advice, and I expect you'll get some help as well. You look to me as if you could use it."

"The castle staff is very good," Mendanbar said stiffly. "And my steward does an excellent job."

"I'm sure he does," Morwen said. "But one good steward isn't enough to run a normal kingdom, much less one like the Enchanted Forest. It's perfectly plain just from looking at you that you're wearing yourself out trying to do everything yourself."

"It is?"

Morwen gave a firm little nod. "It is. And it's quite unnecessary. All you really need—"

"—is a wife," Mendanbar muttered resignedly, recognizing the beginning of Willin's familiar complaint.

"—is someone sensible to talk to," Morwen finished. She looked at him sternly over the tops of her glasses. "Preferably someone who knows at least a little about running a kingdom. An exiled prince, for instance, though they don't usually stay long enough to be useful. Someone who'll do more than make lists of things you need to attend to."

Mendanbar thought of Willin's endless schedules and could not help smiling. "You're probably right." He suppressed a sigh; he didn't have time to spend hunting for a capable adviser. "Do you know anyone suitable?"

"Several people, but they're all quite happy where they are right now," Morwen said. "Don't worry. This is the Enchanted Forest. If you start seriously looking for good help, you'll find some."

"I hope I recognize it when I see it," Mendanbar said. He took another long drink of cider and stared into the mug. "You're the most sensible person I've talked to in days. I don't suppose *you'd* consider moving to the castle?"

"Certainly not," Morwen answered tartly. "I have quite enough to do here. However, I'll have the cats keep an eye out for any more burned-out patches of forest, and if I think of anything that might be important I'll let you know. Finish your cider and go see Kazul before you talk yourself out of it."

"I won't talk myself out of it," Mendanbar said, taking another sip of cider. "It's a good idea." He picked up the dragon scales and put them back into his pocket. He hoped Kazul would be able to tell him something worthwhile. The Enchanted Forest was large, but it could disappear in a hurry if someone started punching holes in it. He frowned suddenly. "Do dragons eat magic?"

"Not that I know of," Morwen said. "Why do you ask?"

"That burned-out place I told you about," Mendanbar said. "There wasn't any magic left in it. It had been sucked dry. I've never seen anything like it."

"I don't think dragons would have done that," Morwen said. She considered for a moment, then rose. "Wait here a minute; I want to look something up."

She walked over to the back door, the one through which Mendanbar had come in. He watched, puzzled, as she opened the door and stepped through into a room full of tall, dark bookcases. Morwen left the door open and disappeared among the shelves. Mendanbar blinked. The windows on either side of the door looked out on the garden, and the one on the right still had a cat in it. *Oh, of course*, he thought. *It's one of those doors that go where you want them to.* There was a door like that in one of the castle attics, which was convenient for getting back to the ground floor without actually climbing down seven flights of stairs. Unfortunately, you still had to climb up all seven flights in order to get to the attic in the first place.

Morwen reappeared, holding a red book with the title *The Patient Dragon* printed on the cover in gold. She closed the library door behind her and sat down at the table again. She flipped rapidly through the book, then slowed and read half a page with great care.

"I thought so," she said. "Dragons don't eat magic. They generate their own, the way unicorns do."

"You're sure?"

"See for yourself." Morwen held the book out. "Austen is very reliable, and the more obscure the fact, the more reliable he tends to be. If he says dragons make their own magic, they do."

"I'll take your word for it," Mendanbar said. "But the more I find out, the less sense any of this makes."

"Then you haven't found out enough," Morwen said.

They talked for a few more minutes while Mendanbar finished his cider. Morwen told him how to find Kazul's cave in the Mountains of Morning but refused to advise him on what to do when he got there. Finally, she packed him off with two bottles of cider, the red book about dragons, and a recommendation not to waste any more time than he had to.

Mendanbar headed straight back to the castle. Visiting the King of the Dragons was going to take more preparation than simply talking to a sensible witch, and Morwen was right about wasting time.

4

In Which a Wizard
Pays a Visit

When Mendanbar got back to the castle, the first person he saw was Willin, standing in the doorway looking relieved. By the time Mendanbar got within earshot, however, the elf's expression had changed to a ferocious scowl.

"I am happy to see that Your Majesty has returned safely," Willin said stiffly. "I was about to send a party out to search for you."

"Willin, that's ridic—" Mendanbar broke off as his brain caught up with him. Willin might fuss and complain about the king playing hooky, but he wouldn't send someone out looking for him without more reason than irritation. "What's happened?"

Willin unbent very slightly. "Your Majesty has an unexpected visitor." He paused. "At least, I presume he is unexpected."

"Don't frown at me like that," Mendanbar said. "*I* certainly didn't expect anyone. If I had, I'd have told you."

"So I had assumed," Willin said, relaxing a little more. "And since Your Majesty is not forgetful, in the normal way of things, I felt sure you would not have,. ah, left the palace so precipitously if you had had an appointment."

"Who is it?" Mendanbar asked. "Not another complaint from the Darkmorning Elves, I hope? If it is, you can tell them I won't see them. I've had enough of their whining, and I've got more important things to attend to right now."

"No," Willin said. "It's Zemenar, the Head Wizard of the Society of Wizards."

"Oh, lord," Mendanbar said. He had only met the Head Wizard once before, at his coronation three years earlier, and he hadn't liked the man much then. Still, the Society of Wizards was a powerful group, and its members were not the sort of people it was a good idea to offend. He ran a hand distractedly through his hair. "How long has he been waiting? What does he want?"

"He's only been here for a few minutes," Willin reassured him. The elf's frown returned. "He refused to tell me his business, Your Majesty. He said it was a matter for Your Majesty's ears alone."

"He would," Mendanbar muttered. "As I recall, he's got an exaggerated idea of his own importance."

"Your Majesty!" said Willin, clearly shocked by such plain speaking. "The Head Wizard of the Society of Wizards is a person of great distinction."

"*He* certainly thinks so," Mendanbar said. "Oh, don't worry, I won't say anything improper when I'm talking to him. Where is he?"

"I asked him to wait in the main audience chamber."

"Good. I'll go see what he wants. You take these down to the kitchen." Mendanbar handed Morwen's jugs of cider to Willin. The elf blinked in puzzled surprise. Before Willin had time to collect himself, Mendanbar grabbed a handful of magic and twisted hard.

The courtyard faded into white mist. An instant later, the mist evaporated, leaving Mendanbar standing in the middle of his study. The wooden gargoyle in the corner immediately began shouting at him.

"You! You've got a lot of nerve, waltzing in as if nothing's happened. I bet you thought that trick with the soapy water was funny! You'll be sorry for it when the wood up here starts to rot from the damp, you wait and see."

"That's why you're there," Mendanbar said as he set the book Morwen had given him on the desk. "You're supposed to let us know if the wood starts to go bad or gets termites, so we can fix it before the castle falls apart."

"And look at the thanks I get," the gargoyle complained. "Water in my ears and soap in my eyes. How do you expect me to do my job if I can't see?"

Mendanbar listened with half an ear while he rummaged through the desk. The gold circlet he wore for official business was in the bottom drawer under a pile of old envelopes and out-of-date invitations to balls, dinners, birthday parties, cricket games, and teas. As he put the circlet on, Mendanbar frowned at the drawer, wondering why he was saving all that useless paper. He resolved for the hundredth time that week to clean everything out someday soon, shoved the drawer closed, and glanced around to make sure he hadn't forgotten anything.

"Are you listening to me?" the gargoyle yelled.

"Of course not," Mendanbar said. "I never do when you're being insulting."

"Insulting? You want insulting? I'll give you insulting. You always dress funny! You've got feet like an elephant! Your nose is too big and your ears stick out!"

"Not much, compared to yours," said Mendanbar cheerfully as he crossed to the door. "Stop grousing; if you can see my nose from up where you are, there's nothing wrong with your eyes."

"Your hair is a bird's nest!" the gargoyle shouted just before the door closed behind Mendanbar. "A bird's nest, do you hear me?"

Mendanbar rolled his eyes and headed down the corridor toward the main audience chamber. He supposed he would have to apologize to the gargoyle sooner or later, unless he could figure out a way to muffle the noise while he worked. Maybe he could enchant a pair of earplugs to keep out the gargoyle's voice and nothing else. A spell that specific would be tricky, but it would be worth it just to see the gargoyle's face when it realized Mendanbar didn't mind its chatter. Mendanbar smiled and pushed open the rear door of the audience chamber.

Zemenar turned as Mendanbar entered, and the blue and gray robes he wore flared out around him. His face was just as sharp and angular as Mendanbar remembered. Giving Mendanbar a long, appraising look, Zemenar bowed his head in greeting. "Your Majesty."

"Welcome, Head Wizard," Mendanbar said, bowing slightly in return. Something tugged gently at his mind, distracting him. The strands of magic, which were always particularly plentiful inside the castle, were drifting slowly toward the staff Zemenar carried. In another minute or two, they would begin winding around Zemenar's staff like thread winding onto a spool. Before long, the wizard's staff would absorb them, leaving a tangled knot in the orderly net of magic, and Mendanbar would have to spend hours straightening it out later.

It happened every time a wizard came to the Enchanted Forest, and it was very inconvenient. Mendanbar had gotten tired of asking wizards to keep their staffs from soaking up magic. They hardly ever understood what he was talking about, and if he did manage to make it clear, they generally got upset and indignant. He didn't want to upset the Head Wizard of the Society of Wizards, but he didn't want to spend his afternoon cleaning up a magical mess in the middle of his castle, either. He reached out with a mental hand and nudged the invisible cords away from the staff.

Zemenar did not seem to notice. "I have come to see you about a matter of much urgency to the Society

46

of Wizards," he said, stroking his long gray beard portentously. "I hope you will be willing to assist us."

"That depends on what kind of help you're asking for," Mendanbar replied. "There are some things I won't do, and a few that I can't. I'm sure you understand."

"Entirely," Zemenar said, though he sounded a little put out, as if he had hoped to get Mendanbar to agree quickly, without asking any awkward questions.

Mendanbar felt like rolling his eyes in exasperation. Everybody who lived in the Enchanted Forest knew better than to make a promise without knowing what they were promising. Did this wizard think that Mendanbar was stupid just because he was young?

"We in the Society of Wizards have been having a great deal of difficulty recently with the dragons in the Mountains of Morning," Zemenar went on. "That is the root of the problem."

"I don't think I can help you with the dragons," Mendanbar said. The strands of magic were drifting toward the wizard's staff again. He gave them another nudge. "The Mountains of Morning aren't part of the Enchanted Forest, so I can't just order the dragons to behave. If you were having trouble with elves, now, I might be able—"

"Naturally, we don't wish to involve you in our dispute," Zemenar interrupted smoothly. "However, one of the results of our quarrel is that the King of the Dragons has cut off the Society's access to the Caves of Fire and Night."

"I still don't see—"

"The caves are the source of many of the ingredients we use in our spells," Zemenar broke in once more. "They are also the only place it is possible to make certain items we need for our research." He paused and blinked, fingering his staff with one hand as if he thought there might be a rough spot somewhere along it and he was trying to find it without attracting attention. "We—the Society of Wizards—must have some way of entering the caves."

"Go on." Mendanbar tried not to sound as irritated as he felt. He did not like Zemenar's lecturing tone, he was tired of being interrupted, and he still did not see what the Society's dispute with the dragons had to do with him. On top of that, the invisible threads of magic were moving toward Zemenar's staff again, almost as if something were sucking them in. Mendanbar yanked at them hard, wishing he could do the same to the Head Wizard.

"That is where you come in, Your Majesty," Zemenar said. He sounded vaguely confused, as if he were trying to concentrate on two things at once. "You, ah, could be of great use . . . that is, you could help us enormously."

"How?" The strands of magic were gliding toward the staff more quickly than ever. Mendanbar could see that if he kept pulling at them he would soon be unable to pay attention to anything else. He thought for a moment, while Zemenar rambled, then he took hold of a fat, invisible cord and with a swift gesture threw it in a loop around Zemenar. The loop hovered three feet from the Head Wizard in all directions, spinning slowly. Other cords floated toward it and glanced off before they came anywhere near Zemenar or his staff. Mendanbar smiled slightly.

The Head Wizard broke off his speech in mid-sentence. "What was that?" he demanded.

"I beg your pardon," Mendanbar said with dignity. "As the ruler of the Enchanted Forest, there are sometimes matters that require my immediate attention. I have dealt with this one."

Zemenar frowned, plainly taken aback. "You have? But I didn't sense any spell—" He stopped short, staring at Mendanbar in consternation.

"You would not," Mendanbar said in an offhand manner. Inwardly, he smiled. Apparently wizards could feel normal spell-casting, but they could not sense Mendanbar's way of doing magic. He wondered why no one had ever mentioned it. Undetectable spells could be a big advantage, if he ever had trouble with the Society of Wizards. "It was not exactly a spell, just something to do with the forest forces. It need not concern you."

"Of course, Your Majesty," Zemenar said after a long pause. "If I may continue?"

"Please do."

"What we are asking is that you allow the wizards of our society to enter the Caves of Fire and Night from the Enchanted Forest," Zemenar said. "There is a way in somewhere along your eastern border, I believe."

"Yes, but it doesn't stay put," Mendanbar pointed out. "Nothing in the Enchanted Forest does, at least, not for long."

"It's always in the same *general* area, though,"

Zemenar said confidently. "We're willing to take whatever time is needed to find it."

Mendanbar thought of the enormous number of knots and tangles that the wizards would cause while they wandered around looking for the entrance to the caves, and he could barely suppress a shudder. "What about the dragons?"

"If you have no authority over them, they can have none over your gateway into the Caves of Fire and Night," Zemenar said, watching Mendanbar closely with his hard, bright eyes.

"That's not what I meant." Mendanbar paused, pretending to consider. "I think I must refuse your request, temporarily at least," he said in as judicious a tone as he could manage. "I have certain . . . differences of my own to settle with the King of the Dragons at the moment. From what you say, the dragons would object if I let your wizards into the Caves of Fire and Night, and I do not want to make my discussion with them any more difficult than it is likely to be already. I hope you understand."

"Ah." A fleeting expression of satisfaction flicked across Zemenar's face. "I am sorry to hear that you, too, are having trouble with dragons. I hope you will be able to settle things suitably. They are sly creatures, you know, and one can never tell what they are thinking."

The same thing could be said about the Head Wizard of the Society of Wizards, thought Mendanbar. "Thank you for your kind wishes," he said aloud.

"If you would like our assistance, the Society of Wizards would be happy to advise you," Zemenar said with a smile. "We have had a great deal of experience with dragons over the years."

"I appreciate the offer," Mendanbar replied cautiously. He did not want to offend the Head Wizard, but he doubted that the wizards' advice would help him much. After all, they seemed to be having more trouble with dragons than he was.

"Have you met the new King of the Dragons or her princess?" the Head Wizard went on.

"No, I—princess?" Mendanbar forgot his misgivings in a wave of surprised dismay. "The King of the Dragons has a princess?"

"She does indeed," Zemenar said. There was a faint frown in his eyes, and his fingers were stroking his staff again. "She's a real troublemaker, too—the princess, I mean. Our misunderstanding with the dragons is all her fault."

"Oh, lord," Mendanbar said. He raised a hand to run his fingers through his hair and remembered just in time that he was wearing his circlet. "And King Kazul listens to her?"

"Certainly. Most of the dragons do, now. Cimorene is quite the power behind the throne in the Mountains of Morning."

There was a sneer in Zemenar's voice, along with a good deal of suppressed anger. Mendanbar couldn't blame him. He'd had enough trouble with princesses himself to know the type. Cimorene must be one of the beautiful, empty-headed, ambitious bores whose only talents were the ability to stare innocently with their blue eyes and a knack for wrapping people—or, in Cimorene's case, dragons—around their fragile fingers. She was probably too stupid to realize how much trouble her manipulations caused, but if she did notice she probably liked having the power to produce turmoil.

"Oh, lord," Mendanbar repeated. Why hadn't Morwen warned him? Well, he had to talk to Kazul, one way or another. Perhaps Morwen had heard about his aversion to princesses and hadn't wanted to give him any reason to put off the visit. Mendanbar looked at Zemenar, completely in charity with the wizard for the first time. "Thank you for telling me."

"You're very welcome," Zemenar said. "You will let me know how things go, won't you? And do remember that the Society of Wizards will be happy to give you whatever help you may need. It's in our own interest, after all. The sooner you get this little matter settled, the sooner you'll be able to reconsider our request about the Caves of Fire and Night."

"Yes, certainly," Mendanbar said. "Is that all, then? I'll have Willin show you out."

"That won't be necessary." Zemenar gave Mendanbar a smile that set Mendanbar's teeth on edge. "I *am* a wizard, after all. Good day, Your Majesty."

Zemenar bowed and was suddenly and completely gone. No, not completely; Mendanbar could feel a lump of magic in the center of the looping spell where Zemenar had been standing. Mendanbar frowned. He might appreciate Zemenar's warning about Kazul's Princess, but that was no reason for the wizard to go leaving leftover bits of magic in his castle.

Mendanbar reached for the loop, to undo it, and

paused. As long as he was at home, he might as well do this the easy way. He twitched a different strand of magic, and the audience chamber dissolved around him.

He materialized in the cool darkness of the castle armory. Lighting the wall torches with another twitch of the magic threads, he looked around. Willin had been hard at work since the last time Mendanbar had visited the armory. Most of the swords and shields that had been piled in one corner or another were now hanging in neat pairs on the walls. Extra swords, spears, maces, lances, and knives hung in closely spaced rows higher up. The effect was almost decorative. Mendanbar made a mental note to compliment Willin, then turned his attention toward the wooden chests along the far wall.

The one he wanted was in the center. He reached into his pocket for the key and realized he had left it in his desk. He sighed and snapped his fingers. With a small pop, the key appeared in the air level with his nose and fell into his palm. Mendanbar smiled at it and bent to open the chest. Willin was always after him to have a proper set of keys made for the various doors and drawers and chests and hiding places in the castle, but Mendanbar couldn't see any reason to waste the effort when the Key to the Castle was all you needed to open any lock in the place.

It wasn't as if Willin needed a spell to call the Key, either, Mendanbar thought as he lifted the lid of the chest. The Key had its own magic. As long as it was inside the castle, it came to whoever called it. Willin just wanted to puff up his own consequence by carrying a big bunch of keys jangling at his belt. Mendanbar looked down and forgot about Willin.

There was only one thing in the chest: a sword, gleaming in the torchlight. It was very plain, almost ordinary-looking, and it didn't have an air of magic about it at all, though anyone who looked at it closely would notice that it shone too brightly and had too sharp an edge to be an ordinary sword. Mendanbar reached in and took the hilt in his hand with a sigh of satisfaction. In the air around him, the unseen strands of power hummed in response, for this sword was linked to the warp and weft of the Enchanted Forest in ways no one, not even the Kings of the Enchanted Forest, really understood. Mendanbar always felt better when he had the sword with him, but he couldn't wear it around the castle all the time. It made Willin unhappy and visitors nervous. So he kept the sword in the armory unless he could think of an excuse to use it.

Rising, he swung the sword twice, just for fun. Then he hunted around until he found a sword belt and scabbard, put the sword in the sheath, and buckled the belt around his waist. With another wave of his hand, he was back in the audience chamber.

5

In Which There Is a Misunderstanding and Mendanbar Does Some Plumbing

*T*he awkward lump of wizard-magic was right where Mendanbar had left it. He studied it for a moment, then drew his sword.

"Your Majesty!" said Willin from the doorway. *"What* are you *doing?"*

"Cleaning up after our visitor," Mendanbar replied. "Do be quiet for a minute, Willin. I need to concentrate."

"But—"

Mendanbar shot an irritated look at Willin. The castle steward broke off and closed his mouth into a thin, disapproving line. Mendanbar waited half a moment longer to make sure the elf was not going to say anything else, then turned back to the lump. Raising the sword, he reached over the loop of Enchanted Forest magic and stuck the point into the center of the mass.

A surge of power ran through the sword as it sucked up the wizard's leftovers and sent them to reinforce the invisible network of Enchanted Forest magic. The surge was stronger than Mendanbar had expected, and he frowned as he lifted the sword away from the now-empty space and put it back in its sheath. Perhaps it hadn't been extra, unused magic, after all; perhaps Zemenar had deliberately left a spell behind. It was too late to test it now, though. The sword was thorough, and whatever the lump had been, it was now gone for good.

"Your Majesty?"

Willin's voice sounded much more tentative than it had a moment before. Mendanbar almost smiled, but Willin was sure to get upset if he thought he was being laughed at. So Mendanbar kept his face stiff and took a little longer than necessary to undo the loop he had left to guard the wizard's magic. When he was positive that his expression was normal, he turned.

"Yes, Willin?"

"What was all that about? Has my lord the Head Wizard gone? Why are you wearing your sword? What—"

"One thing at a time," Mendanbar interrupted gently. "Zemenar has gone, yes. He cast a vanishing spell, and a very good one, too. No smoke, no whirling dust, just *poof* and he was gone. Unfortunately, he wasn't as tidy with the end of his spell, and some of it got left behind. Or at least, that's what I thought until I got rid of it a minute ago."

"I . . . see," Willin said in a tone that meant he didn't. "And that's why you have your sword?"

"Partly." Mendanbar looked at the empty patch of floor where the wizard had been, then shook his head. Whatever Zemenar might have been up to, it would have to wait. "I have to pay a visit to the King of the Dragons."

Willin's face went completely blank. "You what?"

"I'm going to the Mountains of Morning, to see the King of the Dragons," Mendanbar repeated. "And I'm certainly not going without a sword. There are lots of dangerous creatures in those mountains, and some of them wouldn't care that I'm the King of the Enchanted Forest, even if they bothered to stop for an introduction before they attacked."

"But you can't just *leave*, Your Majesty!" Willin said. "A formal embassy to the King of the Dragons will take weeks to arrange. You'll want a full escort, and—"

"I don't think there's time," Mendanbar broke in, before Willin could get too involved in planning. "Something's come up, and it needs to be dealt with *now*. So I'm going today, in another minute, and you're in charge of the castle until I get back." In a sudden inspiration, Mendanbar pulled the Key to the Castle out of his pocket and handed it ceremoniously to Willin.

"I am deeply honored by Your Majesty's confidence," Willin said. "But are you sure this is necessary?"

"Yes," Mendanbar said. "Oh, and don't let any wizards in while I'm gone. Something funny is going on, and I don't want any of them inside the castle until I figure out what, especially if I'm not here."

"But what should I tell them, if they ask for you?"

"I don't care, as long as you don't let them in," Mendanbar replied. "Is that all? Then I'm going."

He took hold of a strand of magic and pulled. When the misty whiteness cleared away, he was standing among the trees of the Enchanted Forest just outside the castle. With a bit more care, he chose another magic thread and pulled again, harder. This time, he appeared at the very edge of the forest, where the Mountains of Morning began. Two paces in front of him, the vibrant green moss stopped as if it had been sliced away, and the dry gray rock began. He checked to make sure this was the right place—Morwen's directions had been very specific—and then, reluctantly, stepped over the boundary.

Mendanbar had not left the Enchanted Forest for over three years, not since he had become King, and he had forgotten how very barren everything felt outside. He could still sense the free-floating network of magic behind him, but where he stood, the air was empty. Thin grass and scrubby bushes grew in patches wherever dirt had accumulated in low spots and cracks and corners. Ahead, the mountains rose high and sharp and dead. Many magical creatures lived here, but the Mountains of Morning had no magic of their own. Mendanbar could feel the emptiness where the magic should have been, and he shivered in spite of himself.

"At least I don't have to worry about finding Kazul," he told himself. "As long as I don't get my directions mixed up, I should be able to walk straight to her cave." He smiled suddenly. "And it will still be there when I get to it!" That was worth something. And he still had some of the magic of the Enchanted Forest along with him in the form of his sword. Even through the sheath, Mendanbar could feel the reassuring pulse of power.

"Well, there's no sense in putting it off." He shrugged, took a last look back at his forest, and started walking.

Once he got used to the dry, dead, magicless feel of the mountains, Mendanbar actually enjoyed the walk. Much as he loved the Enchanted Forest, he had to admit that it was nice to see so much sky. Since dragons liked high places, the walk was mostly uphill, but that was fun, too. With no trees to block the view, Mendanbar could see for miles, and the higher he got, the more he could see. The hills in the Enchanted Forest tended to be either low, rolling bumps that you hardly noticed, or steep mounds that were usually home to something dangerous, or magical, or both. Most of the latter were made of something strange, too—jasper or polished coal or solid silver. There was even one made of glass somewhere along the southern edge of the forest. Some king had built it in order to get rid of his daughter.

Daughter. King's daughter. Princess! Mendanbar's good mood vanished. He'd forgotten about Kazul's princess.

"And I'll have to be particularly polite to her, no

matter how irritating she is," he reminded himself gloomily. If she had as much influence as Zemenar hinted, she could make things very difficult if she took a dislike to him. He wondered why Kazul had kept her. The King of the Dragons didn't normally bother with a princess, or at least, Mendanbar had never before heard of one who did.

He came around a curve and saw the mouth of a cave in front of him. There was a wide, flat, sandy space in front of the cave, big enough for several dragons to land at the same time, if they were careful about it. The mountain rose straight up behind the cave mouth. Set in the stone over the center of the opening was an outline of a spiky black crown.

As Mendanbar drew nearer, he saw a tarnished brass handle sticking out of a small hole beside the cave. The handle was level with his waist, and next to it was a sign that read: "WELCOME TO THE CAVE OF THE DRAGON KING. Pull handle to ring bell." On the line below, someone had added in neat letters printed in bright red paint, "ABSOLUTELY NO wizards, salespeople, or rescuers. This means YOU."

Mendanbar stared at the sign for a minute and began to smile. No wonder Zemenar didn't like Kazul's princess. Well, he wasn't a wizard, he wasn't selling anything, and he certainly didn't want to rescue anybody. He gave the handle a pull.

Somewhere inside the cave, a bell rang. "Well, it's about time," said a woman's voice, and Mendanbar's heart sank. He heard footsteps coming toward the mouth of the cave, and the same voice continued,

"I was hoping you'd get here before I left. The sink is—"

The speaker came out of the cave, took a look at Mendanbar, and broke off in midsentence. "Oh, no, not *another* one," she said.

Mendanbar stared at her in utter bafflement. If this was a princess, she was like no princess he had ever seen, and he had seen dozens. True, she had a small gold crown pinned into her hair, and she was very pretty—beautiful, in fact—but she was wearing a blue-and-white checked apron with large pockets. Mendanbar had never seen a princess in an apron before. The dress under the apron was rust-colored and practical-looking, and she had the sleeves rolled up above her elbows. He had never seen a princess with her sleeves rolled up, either. Her jet black hair hung in plain braids almost to her knees, instead of making a cloud of curls around her face. Her eyes were black, too, and she was as tall as Mendanbar.

"Well?" she said in an exasperated tone. "Are you going to stand there like a lump, or are you going to tell me what you want? Although I think I already know."

"Excuse me," Mendanbar said. He pulled himself together and bowed uncertainly. "I think there's been some sort of mistake. I'm looking for Kazul, the King of the Dragons."

"I'll bet you are," the young woman muttered. "Well, you can't have her. I handle my own knights and princes."

"I beg your pardon?" Mendanbar said, blinking.

He was beginning to think the mistake was his. This young woman didn't look like a princess (except for the crown), she didn't act like a princess, and she didn't talk like a princess. But if she wasn't a princess, what was she doing here?

"I handle my own knights," she repeated. "You see, I don't want to be rescued, and it would be silly for someone to get hurt fighting Kazul when I intend to stay here no matter what happens. Besides, Kazul has enough to do being King of the Dragons without people interrupting her to fight for no reason."

"You really *are* Kazul's princess"—what had Zemenar said her name was? Oh, yes—"Cimorene?"

"Yes, of course. Look, I haven't got time to argue about this, not today. Could you please go away and come back in, oh, a week or so, when things are a little more settled? Or I can direct you to a more cooperative princess, if you'd rather not wait. Marchak has a very nice one just now, and he lives quite close by."

"No, I'm afraid not," Mendanbar said. He was beginning to think Willin had been right to say he should wait for a formal audience. "You see, I didn't come to rescue you, or anybody. I'm the King of the Enchanted Forest, and I really did come to talk to Kazul. And it's urgent. So—"

"Oh, drat," said Cimorene. "Are you sure it can't wait? Kazul isn't here right now."

"I'll wait for her," Mendanbar said with polite firmness. "As I said, the matter is urgent."

Cimorene frowned suddenly. "Did you say you were the King of the *Enchanted Forest*?"

Mendanbar nodded. "My name is Mendanbar."

"Just why is it that you're so eager to see Kazul, Your Majesty?" Cimorene said suspiciously.

"I ran across a . . . problem in the Enchanted Forest this morning," Mendanbar replied, choosing his words with care. "A witch named Morwen advised me to talk to the King of the Dragons about it."

"*Morwen* sent you?" Cimorene looked surprised, then thoughtful. "It must be all right, then. Come in and sit down, and I'll see if I can explain."

"As you wish, Princess," Mendanbar said, bowing.

"Just call me Cimorene," she said, leading Mendanbar into the cave. She bent to pick up a lantern from the floor inside the entrance and added, "My official title now is Chief Cook and Librarian, so I've gotten out of the habit of being called 'Princess.' "

"Chief Cook and Librarian?" Mendanbar said curiously. "How did that happen?"

"Kazul and I decided on it between us after she became King of the Dragons last year," Cimorene said. "You see, the King of the Dragons doesn't usually have a princess, and we didn't want the other dragons grumbling about Kazul breaking with tradition. I was hoping it would discourage the knights a bit, too."

"Oh?"

"Well, it doesn't sound particularly noble and knightly to say you've rescued the Chief Cook and Librarian, does it? And it has cut down on the number of interruptions. I used to get two or three knights a day, and now there's only about one a week. And the ones who *do* come are at least smart enough to figure out that I'm still a princess even if the dragons call me Chief Cook."

"Doesn't that make them harder to get rid of?"

"Not at all. The smart ones listen when I argue with them. The stupid ones think I'm kidding. I had to offer to fight a couple of them myself before I could get them to go away."

Mendanbar peered doubtfully at Cimorene in the dim lantern-light. She didn't look as if she were joking. "You actually offered to fight a knight?"

"Four of them," Cimorene said, nodding. "*And* a prince. It was the only way to convince them." She looked at Mendanbar uncertainly. "I'm sorry if I behaved badly to you at first, but I really did think you were here to rescue me. It's the crown." She pointed to the circlet on his head. "You wouldn't believe the trouble I've had with some of the princes. Being rude is the only way to get rid of them in a hurry, and sometimes even that doesn't work. Especially if they're particularly stupid."

"I understand," Mendanbar said without thinking. "They sound a lot like princesses—stubborn, witless, and—" He stopped short in dismay. He'd forgotten for a moment that Cimorene was a princess, too. He hoped she wouldn't be insulted.

Fortunately, Cimorene didn't seem insulted at all. She nodded. "Exactly. That's why I send the knights and princes on to rescue other princesses. They mostly deserve each other. Of course, I *do* try to make sure I send the nicest knights to the nicest princesses. They can't help it if they're silly."

They had reached a side opening, and Cimorene hesitated. Then she shrugged and went in. "The kitchen's a mess today," she said over her shoulder, "but even when it's messy, it's more comfortable for human-type people than the big caves where the dragons go to chat. I can make tea, too, if you'd like some."

Before he could answer, Mendanbar emerged from the side tunnel into a large, well-lit cavern. An enormous black stove took up half of one wall, and the other walls were lined with tall wooden cupboards. A stone sink next to the door was filled to the brim with scummy gray water, and the shelf next to it was overflowing with dirty dishes. In the middle of the floor stood a large wooden table and three mismatched chairs.

"Tea sounds good," Mendanbar said, politely ignoring the dishes.

Cimorene scowled at the sink and began rummaging through the cupboards. "Do you mind having your tea in a wine glass? I know it's a little strange, but I'm afraid all the cups are dirty. The sink has been plugged up for nearly a week, and I haven't been able to do the dishes."

"I don't mind," Mendanbar said. "But you'll have to do something about that sink sooner or later, you know."

"I've tried," Cimorene said in an irritated tone. "Do you have any idea how hard it is to persuade a plumber to come look at a dragon's sink? I thought I'd finally found one, but he was supposed to get here yesterday morning and still hasn't shown up, so he's probably not coming. And there aren't any books on plumbing in Kazul's library, or I'd have fixed it myself."

"I'm sorry," Mendanbar said. "Maybe I can do something about it."

"Go ahead," Cimorene replied. "You can't make it any worse than it is already."

That didn't sound like much of a vote of confidence to Mendanbar, but it didn't matter. He went over to the sink and studied it for a moment, then backed up a pace and drew his sword.

Cimorene made a startled noise. "Your sword does plumbing?" she said, sounding interested. "I knew it was magic, but I thought it was for dragons."

"It does most things," Mendanbar said absently. Working magic outside the Enchanted Forest took a lot of concentration. He squinted down the length of the blade at the sink, feeling the power within the sword tingle against his palm. Then he whipped the sword through the air, pushing power out of it to wrap around the sink. With a final flourish, he touched the tip of the sword to the surface of the scummy water. There was a spray of magic, a loud glug, and the water swirled and began to run down the drain.

"There," said Mendanbar. "That should do it." He wiped the tip of his sword and stuck it back in its sheath.

"It certainly should!" Cimorene said. "Is your magic always that flashy?"

"What do you mean?"

"Never mind. I'll wash some cups while the tea water is boiling. Sit down while I get the kettle started."

Mendanbar sat down at the table and frowned suddenly. "Oh, bother."

"What?"

"Morwen gave me some cider to bring to King

Kazul, and I was so busy cleaning up after Zemenar that I forgot to pick it up before I left. I'm sorry. I'll have to send it with someone when I get back."

Cimorene stopped short, holding the teakettle suspended in midair. "Zemenar? Not the Head Wizard of the Society of Wizards?"

"Yes, of course," Mendanbar said, a little surprised by her reaction. Then he recalled how much Zemenar seemed to dislike Cimorene. Presumably Cimorene felt the same way about Zemenar.

"And you had to clean up after him? It figures," Cimorene muttered. She finished filling the kettle and put it on the stove, then went back to the sink and washed two cups, two saucers, and two spoons with an intense concentration that made it obvious she was thinking about something else.

Mendanbar was happy to let her think. He had a few things to mull over himself. Cimorene was not at all what he'd expected. She acted more like Morwen than like a princess. He wondered where she had come from and how she had gotten captured by the dragons. He nearly asked, but pulled himself up short before the words left his mouth. He hadn't come to talk to a princess. No, indeed. "When will King Kazul be back?" he asked instead.

Cimorene did not answer at once. She set the teacups on the table, poured hot water into the teapot to brew, and sat down across from Mendanbar. She studied him for a long minute, then gave a decisive nod.

"All right," she said. "I'll tell you the truth. I don't know."

A wave of irritation swept over Mendanbar. "If Kazul didn't tell you when she expected to be back, why didn't you say so at once?"

"Oh, she told me," Cimorene said. She looked very sober. "She was supposed to be home the day before yesterday."

"And she's not back yet?"

Cimorene nodded again. "And she hasn't sent a message or anything. She's disappeared. I was just getting ready to go search for her when you showed up."

6

In Which Mendanbar and Cimorene Have a Long Talk and Mendanbar Reluctantly Decides to Embark on a Journey

*M*endanbar took a deep breath. "I think you'd better tell me everything you know about this," he said. "When did Kazul leave, and where was she going?"

"She left last Monday," Cimorene replied readily. "She was going to visit her grandchildren in the northern part of the mountains. She does that whenever she gets a chance, and sometimes she stays a few extra days, but she's *always* sent word before when she's done that." She frowned worriedly.

"I—grandchildren?"

Cimorene smiled. "I know. I was taken aback when I found out about them, too. You just don't think of the King of the Dragons as a doting grandmother, but she is. In fact, I suspect she took longer than she had to about the negotiations with the Frost Giants up there, just so she'd have an excuse to stay a few more days. Anyway, she was planning to spend a couple of days with them and then swing through the Enchanted Forest on her way home."

"She was coming to see me?" Mendanbar asked, surprised.

"Not exactly." Cimorene hesitated. "We'd heard that someone was growing dragonsbane in one of the valleys along the border, and she wanted to see whether it was true. You can see why I'm worried."

"Growing dragonsbane—you mean, deliberately planting it? There have always been a few patches of the stuff here and there."

"The way we heard it, this was an entire valley full. That's hardly accidental." Cimorene lifted the lid of the teapot and peered inside, then poured a cup for each of them. "Kazul wanted to check for herself, quietly, before any of the younger dragons heard about it. Some of them are . . . impulsive. She didn't want someone tearing off in a fury to burn down the Enchanted Forest with no more reason than a rumor."

"Oh, lord." Mendanbar pushed his hair backward off his forehead and grimaced at his tea. "I'll bet that's what happened. I wish she'd sent word to me."

Cimorene studied her cup with unnecessary thoroughness. "She was afraid you might be the one doing it."

"*Me?*"

"The King of the Enchanted Forest. You haven't been particularly friendly since she took over, you know." She frowned suddenly. "Why *did* you turn up today, anyway? And what did you mean, 'that's what happened'? Don't tell me somebody really *has* started setting fire to the Enchanted Forest!"

"Almost," Mendanbar said. He explained about the dead area and the dragon scales he had found. "Morwen said that they were all from the same dragon, but they had been enchanted to look as if they came from several different dragons. I was hoping King Kazul would tell me which dragon they belonged to, and maybe let me ask him a few questions."

"Let me look at them," Cimorene said.

Mendanbar took the scales out of his pocket and spread them out on the table.

Cimorene made a face. "I can tell you whose scales they were, all right, but I'm afraid it won't help much. Woraug isn't around any more."

"It's a start," Mendanbar said. "You're sure these are his?"

"Very sure. But I'm afraid you won't be able to ask him any questions." Cimorene smiled, as if at some private joke.

"Why not?"

"Because the reason Woraug isn't around any more is that he got turned into a toad about a year ago. Do you know how the King of the Dragons is chosen?"

"By a test," Mendanbar replied, a little puzzled by the question. "When a king dies, the crown goes to whichever dragon can carry Colin's Stone from the Ford of Whispering Snakes to the Vanishing Mountain."

"Yes. Well, Woraug poisoned the old King of the Dragons. Then he arranged with the Society of Wizards to rig the test so he'd be the next King," Cimorene said

71

matter-of-factly. "It was mostly luck that we found out in time to stop them. When we did, Woraug turned into a toad because of his un-dragonlike behavior." She sipped at her tea. "I think a snake ate him," she added thoughtfully.

There were so many things Mendanbar wanted to say in response to this disturbing summary that for a moment he couldn't say anything at all. He took a large swallow of tea, which gave him an extra minute to think. "Is *that* why the wizards have been banned from the Mountains of Morning?" he managed at last.

"Of course," Cimorene answered. "Kazul couldn't do anything more. Even though we knew it was all their idea, it was Woraug who actually poisoned the King. Didn't Morwen tell you about it? She was there."

"No," Mendanbar said. "It didn't come up." He shook his head. "No wonder Zemenar didn't want to talk about why the dragons don't want wizards in the mountains anymore."

Cimorene nodded. "The wizards don't talk about it because their scheme didn't work out, and the dragons don't talk about it because the wizards came so close that the dragons are embarrassed to admit it. And Morwen is too discreet to spread the story around when the dragons would rather she didn't."

"I see." Mendanbar saw considerably more than that. The disagreement between the dragons and the Society of Wizards was not a minor matter, as Zemenar had led him to believe. And Kazul's princess—or rather, Chief Cook and Librarian, he reminded himself—was nothing like the sneaky, manipulative girl Zemenar had hinted she was, either. It looked very much as if Zemenar had been deliberately trying to cause trouble between Mendanbar and the dragons, or at least get Mendanbar off to a bad start with their King. He wondered what Zemenar would have said about Morwen if *her* name had come up.

"It wouldn't surprise me if the Society of Wizards was behind this, too," Cimorene said, waving her hand at the scales. "It's exactly the kind of twisty scheme they'd come up with."

"It's possible," Mendanbar acknowledged, "but why would they want to bring the Enchanted Forest into their argument with the dragons?"

"Maybe they think you'll clean the dragons out of the mountains, or at least reduce their numbers enough so that the wizards will be able to come through without getting eaten."

Mendanbar shook his head. "If it came to a fight, the Enchanted Forest and the Mountains of Morning would be very evenly matched. A war would cut the wizards off from both places as long as there was any fighting, and it would probably drag on for ages. Zemenar must know that. He'd have to have an awfully good reason to start something like that."

"Maybe he does."

"Maybe, but I can't think what it could be. Can you?"

"No," Cimorene admitted. "But if I figure it out, I'll let you know."

"Meanwhile, is there anyone else who could have done this?" Mendanbar asked, waving at the line of scales on the table.

"There aren't many people who can get hold of

even one dragon scale, much less five from the same dragon," Cimorene said, scowling at the table. "Woraug's princess might have kept one or two as a souvenir, but I don't think she'd have had this many, and anyway she doesn't know any magic." Suddenly she looked up. "Wait a minute! When Woraug turned into a toad, a whole batch of scales fell off and scattered."

"What happened to them?"

"We just left them at the ford," Cimorene said with a shrug. "Nobody thought it was important. Most of them are probably still there. Dragon scales last a long time."

"At the Ford of Whispering Snakes?" Mendanbar asked. Cimorene nodded, and he grimaced. "Then anyone who walked by could have picked up these scales any time in the past year. That doesn't narrow things down much."

"I'm as sorry about that as you are," Cimorene said.

Mendanbar's face must have shown his surprise, because she gave him an exasperated look and went on, "Hadn't it occurred to you that we'd want to know who's plotting to get dragons blamed for their mischief? Especially if it turns out *not* to be the Society of Wizards."

"But—oh. If it's *not* the Society, then you have a new enemy you don't know anything about."

Cimorene nodded again, very soberly. "I just wish I had time to look into it right now, but with Kazul missing it will have to wait."

"You'll let me know when she gets back?"

"I'll tell Roxim to send you word if she shows up

74

while I'm gone," Cimorene assured him. "And if I find her first, I'll tell her everything you've told me. I'm sure she'll get in touch with you right away."

"Thank you."

"Now, is there anything else you want to know? Because if there isn't, I need to be going," Cimorene went on. "It's a long walk to Flat Top Mountain, and I'd like to get there before dark."

"Surely you don't plan to walk all the way to the northern end of the Mountains of Morning." He was surprised and suddenly disappointed by this evidence of princesslike behavior. From their brief acquaintance, he'd thought Cimorene had better sense.

"Of course not," Cimorene replied impatiently. "I'm not stupid. I'm going to borrow a magic carpet from Ballimore, the giantess who lives on Flat Top Mountain."

Mendanbar choked on the last of his tea. "Do you expect a giantess to loan you a carpet just because you have a dragon with you?" he demanded when he could talk again.

"I'd better not, since I won't have a dragon with me," Cimorene retorted. "Not that it's any of your business."

"You're going to wander around the Mountains of Morning *alone* looking for King Kazul?" Mendanbar said, appalled.

"Exactly. And if I can't find her there, I'll swing through the Enchanted Forest on the way back, just the way she was planning to. And it's time I got started, so if you'll just—"

"Oh, no." Mendanbar set his teacup down so emphatically that it rattled the saucer. "If you're fool enough to travel through the Mountains of Morning without a companion, that's not my concern, but you are *not* going through the Enchanted Forest alone. It's too dangerous."

"I can take care of myself," Cimorene snapped. "You forget, I've been living with the dragons for over a year."

"Maybe so," Mendanbar said, trying hard to hold on to his temper. "But the Enchanted Forest is very different from the Mountains of Morning. And what do you suppose will happen if the King of the Dragons's princess—or Cook and Librarian, or whatever— gets captured or killed or enchanted going through *my* forest?"

Cimorene opened her mouth to reply, then paused. "Oh," she said in a very different tone. "Oh, I see. That would cause just the sort of trouble we're both trying to avoid, wouldn't it? I'm sorry. I'm used to people objecting to things because they think I can't do them or shouldn't do them. It didn't occur to me that you might have a *real* reason."

"Then you won't go?" Mendanbar said with relief.

"I have to," Cimorene said in the tones of one explaining something obvious. "It's my job. Besides, Kazul is my friend. I'll just have to make sure I don't get captured or killed or enchanted, that's all."

"It's not as easy as you make it sound."

"I know. I've visited Morwen a time or two," Cimorene said. "I'll manage, one way or another."

76

Mendanbar started to object again, then stopped. He didn't think Cimorene was quite as sure of herself as she sounded, but she was plainly determined to go hunting for Kazul. Well, she was right about one thing: *somebody* had to find the King of the Dragons, and soon. Mendanbar didn't like to think of what might happen if Kazul stayed missing for long, especially if rumors about dragonsbane in the Enchanted Forest started floating around the mountains.

"Is there anyone you can take with you?" Mendanbar asked.

"No," Cimorene said. "Roxim and Marchak are the only dragons who have enough sense not to go off in fits when they hear that Kazul is missing. Roxim is too old for adventures, and Marchak has to stay and take care of business while I'm gone. And I hope you're not going to suggest I borrow Marchak's princess."

"I wouldn't dream of it," Mendanbar said sincerely. "Is she very awful?"

"Actually, she's one of the nice ones," Cimorene admitted. "But she's very silly. She'd try, but she wouldn't enjoy it at all, and she'd be much more of a nuisance than she's worth. I'd rather take my chances alone."

"That's almost as bad an idea as taking that princess along," Mendanbar said. He sighed. "I suppose I'll have to come with you myself."

Cimorene stared at him blankly for a moment, then began to giggle.

"It isn't funny," Mendanbar said. "I mean it." He felt a little hurt by Cimorene's reaction. He wasn't necessarily stuffy or useless or a nuisance to travel with just because he was the King of the Enchanted Forest. Cimorene ought to realize that. After all, he'd fixed the sink for her, hadn't he?

"I know you mean it," Cimorene said when she could talk again. "It wasn't what you said, it was the way you said it." She shook her head, chuckling. "You sound about as eager to come with me as I am to have company. Which isn't much."

"Maybe not, but somebody—"

"What was that?" Cimorene interrupted, holding up a hand for silence.

"I didn't hear anything," Mendanbar said.

"Shhh," Cimorene hissed. She rose and tiptoed to the door, listening. In the quiet, Mendanbar heard a faint thud outside. Cimorene's lips tightened. "Princes or wizards?" she muttered. "Wizards, I'll bet. Princes are noisier."

Still frowning, she picked up the bucket of soapy water that was sitting beside the door. As she reached for the doorknob, Mendanbar started after her. Cimorene hadn't asked for his help, but a bucket of soapy water wasn't much of a weapon against a wizard. If it was a wizard.

The corridor outside the kitchen was pitch black. Cimorene vanished into the gloom, moving with the calm sureness of long familiarity. Cursing mentally, Mendanbar picked his way after her, one hand on the cave wall for guidance, the other stretched out in front of him to keep him from running into anything.

Another muffled crash echoed from up ahead. Mendanbar took two more steps and his outstretched arm touched Cimorene's shoulder. A moment later, Cimorene's voice said calmly, "Phrazelspitz."

Mendanbar felt magic rise around him. Light flared from the walls, then settled into a steady glow, revealing an enormous cavern. He and Cimorene stood in one of five dark openings spaced unevenly around the wall. Halfway across the cave, a tall man in blue and brown wizard's robes stood hanging onto a staff and trying to squint in all directions at once. His hair and beard were brown, and he bore a strong resemblance to Zemenar, only younger.

"Antorell," Cimorene said in tones of disgust. "I might have guessed."

"I'm glad to see you again, Princess Cimorene," the wizard said in an oily tone. "But who could fail to rejoice at the sight of so lovely a princess?"

"What are you doing here?" Cimorene demanded. Mendanbar was pleased to note that she didn't sound at all mollified by Antorell's flattery. "And how did you get in without being eaten?"

"Oh, we wizards have our little ways," Antorell said airily. "And I came because—well, because I was concerned about you, Princess."

"I'll bet," Cimorene muttered. "What do you mean?" she said in a louder voice.

"I thought you might need a friend." Antorell's voice oozed sincerity. "Especially after what Father said when he came back from the Enchanted Forest. If King Mendanbar really is getting ready for a war with the dragons . . ."

"Where did your father get that idea?" Cimorene asked in tones of mild interest.

Antorell frowned slightly, as if he had hoped for a stronger reaction. "Something the King said to him, I think. I shouldn't have repeated it, I suppose, but I was carried away by my feelings."

"Sure you were," Cimorene said. "That's why you sneaked in here without knocking and went blundering around in the dark, instead of calling me or at least bringing a lamp."

"I didn't want to disturb King Kazul, if she happened to be here," Antorell said stiffly.

Cimorene snorted. "If you'd really thought Kazul was here, you wouldn't have come at all. She doesn't like it when people ignore her rules. One of which, may I remind you, was that wizards aren't allowed in the Mountains of Morning anymore."

"But if there's going to be a war—"

"There isn't," Mendanbar said, stepping forward into the light. "At least, not if I can help it. Why are you people trying so hard to make trouble, anyway?"

Antorell's eyes widened, and he sucked in his breath. "Mendanbar? You'll ruin everything, blast you." He smiled a sudden, nasty smile. "Unless I deal with both of you now. Oh, yes, that will do very well. Father will be so pleased."

He raised his staff. Mendanbar started toward him, pulling his sword free as he ran, though he knew the wizard was much too far away to reach before he finished the spell. Cimorene followed quickly, not quite running, carrying her bucket carefully to avoid spilling. They had only gone a few steps when a swirl of smoke appeared in the air in front of them.

The smoke thickened rapidly, then congealed with

shocking suddenness into the largest nightshade Mendanbar had ever seen. It was two feet taller than Mendanbar and covered with spikes of coarse black fur. Its beady black eyes glared at him as it raised a long arm and clicked its dark purple claws together. It hissed, showing a mouthful of fangs.

"There!" cried Antorell over the nightshade's noise. "Vanquish that, Cimorene—if you can!"

7

In Which a Wizard Makes a Mess
and the Journey Begins

*I*gnoring Antorell, Mendanbar kept his eyes on the nightshade. He had a moment's useless wish that he were in the Enchanted Forest, where he could have disposed of the monster with relative ease. Here, things were going to be a lot more complicated. He shifted his grip on the sword and pulled at the power within it.

The nightshade swung at him, its fully extended claws carving a whistling arc in the air. It was very, very fast. Mendanbar barely managed to block in time. The force of the blow knocked him to one side, and he almost lost hold of the sword. The nightshade hissed in pain and shook its arm, but Mendanbar knew it was not seriously hurt. Without active magic behind it, the most damage the sword could have inflicted on a night-shade this big was a bruise.

Again he pulled at the power in the sword, then had to roll to avoid another swing by the nightshade. This time he kept on rolling until he was out of the monster's reach. He came up on one knee and pointed the sword at the nightshade, pushing power through the sword in the pattern he had pictured in his mind.

Antorell's staff struck him across the shoulders. The sword flew out of his hands and he went sprawl-ing. His half-formed spell spun wildly in the air and then was sucked away. He heard an angry shriek from Cimorene, then a shout: "Mendanbar! Dodge left, quick!"

Without hesitation, Mendanbar threw himself to his left. He heard a rush of wind as the nightshade's claws missed him by inches. There was a splash some-where behind him, and Antorell's voice cried, "No! No! You'll be sorry for this, Cimorene!" Then Mendanbar's hand closed on the hilt of his sword. He twisted and brought the sword up, shoving power through it recklessly.

The blast of barely formed magic caught the night-shade in midleap. The creature hung frozen in the air for an instant, then dissolved in a cloud of bright sparks. Mendanbar seized the remnants of magic and pulled them together into a tight knot, ready to throw at another nightshade or at Antorell himself. Only then did he pause to look around.

Cimorene stood a little way away, swinging the empty bucket in one hand and looking at him as if she were impressed in spite of herself.

Antorell had vanished.

"You really *do* like flashy magic," Cimorene commented as Mendanbar climbed warily to his feet. "I haven't seen anything like that since Kazul's coronation party."

"Where's Antorell?" Mendanbar asked. "Did he get away?"

"No," Cimorene said, waving her free hand at a damp area of floor to Mendanbar's right. "I melted him."

"*Melted* him?" Mendanbar looked at the damp patch more closely. Antorell's soggy robes were plastered to the floor in the middle of a gooey puddle. His staff lay along one side of the robes, half-in, half-out of the goo. There was no other trace of him. Mendanbar was impressed, and said so.

"It's really not hard," Cimorene said. "All it takes is a bucket of soapy water with a little lemon juice in it. A friend of mine discovered by accident how to do it, and I've kept a bucket ready ever since, just in case."

"I thought that only worked on witches."

Cimorene shrugged. "Lots of things don't work the way they're supposed to. Morwen's a witch, but she certainly doesn't melt in a bucket of soapy water."

Mendanbar thought of the shining stone step and the spotless wooden floor in Morwen's house, and nodded. "I can see that. But why does it work for wizards?"

"We don't know." Cimorene gave him a sidelong look. "I'm sorry I let Antorell wallop you with his staff, but I didn't want to throw the water at him while you were in the way."

"Why—oh, you mean you were afraid it would

melt me, too?" Mendanbar blinked. "But I'm not a wizard."

"You work magic," Cimorene pointed out. "And I don't know how strict the soapy-water-and-lemon-juice trick is about defining wizards. It would cause a lot of trouble if I melted the King of the Enchanted Forest in the middle of Kazul's living room, even if it isn't permanent."

"You mean he'll be back?" Mendanbar had started to put his sword back in its sheath, but he stopped at once. "How soon?"

"Not for a couple of days, at least," Cimorene reassured him. "Antorell may be Zemenar's son, but he's never been a very good wizard."

"Antorell is the son of the Head Wizard?" Mendanbar shot a considering look at the puddle and the pile of soggy robes. "So that's what he meant when he said his father would be pleased."

"Probably." Cimorene frowned pensively at Antorell's staff. "I've *got* to find Kazul. The Society of Wizards is up to something for sure, and she needs to know right away."

"Couldn't Antorell have come here on his own?" Mendanbar asked, although he didn't really believe it himself.

Cimorene shook her head. "I don't think he'd have dared. As I said, he's not a very good wizard. He wouldn't have been able to keep himself concealed from the dragons, and he certainly must have had help to make anything as nasty and complex as that construct you took care of."

"That wasn't a construct," Mendanbar said. "That

was a nightshade. They're fairly common in parts of the Enchanted Forest. Antorell didn't make it, he just snatched it from somewhere nearby."

"Snatched it?" Cimorene's eyes widened. "Yes, I suppose he could have managed that. I begin to see what you meant about traveling in the Enchanted Forest alone," she added in a thoughtful tone.

"I should hope so," Mendanbar muttered, turning away. "Then you've changed your mind about going?" he added hopefully over his shoulder.

"No, just about whether I accept your offer of escort," Cimorene said. "It'll probably be a nuisance, but nightshades would be much worse."

Slightly startled by this unflattering comparison, Mendanbar glanced back at Cimorene. There was a decided twinkle in her eyes. Mendanbar smiled and bowed elaborately. "Thank you for your kind words, Princess."

"You're welcome, Your Majesty," Cimorene said, curtsying in response. "Now, we'd better get to work, or we'll never get this mess cleaned up in time to get to Flat Top Mountain before dark."

Cleaning up the large cave took less time than Mendanbar had expected, despite the unpleasantly gummy look of the goo that Antorell had left behind. A large part of the mess turned out to be leftover soapy water, which was very convenient. Cimorene mopped most of it up with Antorell's robe, then wrapped the robe around the staff and started toward the rear of the cave.

"What are you going to do with that?" Mendanbar asked curiously.

"Hide it," Cimorene said. "There's not much else you can do to a wizard's staff. They won't break, and even dragon fire won't burn them. I know because we tried everything we could think of the last time we melted some wizards."

"We?"

"Morwen and I. Antorell will get it back eventually, of course, but hiding it will slow him down a little." She left to dispose of the staff while Mendanbar scraped up the last of the goo.

The kitchen was another matter. Cimorene insisted on doing all of the dishes that had been waiting for the sink to get unplugged, which took a while. Mendanbar offered to use his magic on the dishes, but Cimorene politely declined.

"A magic sword that does plumbing is unusual but very useful," she explained as she filled the sink. "A magic sword that does dishes is just plain silly. Besides, there have been two big flares of magic in this cave in the past hour already, and if there's a third one, someone might come to see what I'm up to."

"I didn't notice anything remarkable when Antorell brought the nightshade in," Mendanbar said, frowning. "Though I'll admit I overdid it a little when I got rid of the thing. I was in a hurry."

"Yes, of course," said Cimorene, setting a clean plate on the drain board. "But you weren't in a hurry when you unclogged the sink, were you? That was the other flare I meant, not Antorell's fiddling."

"What was conspicuous about that?" Mendanbar asked defensively. He picked up a clean towel and began drying plates. "It was a perfectly ordinary spell."

Cimorene looked at him. "Right. Just like that sword is a perfectly ordinary magic sword."

"Well, I wouldn't call it *ordinary*, exactly, but that's because it's linked with the Enchanted Forest," Mendanbar said. "Outside of that, it's nothing special."

"Nothing special." Cimorene stopped washing dishes for a moment to stare at him. Suddenly, she frowned. "You mean it. You really haven't noticed."

"Noticed what?"

"The way that sword of yours positively reeks of magic," Cimorene said. "We're going to have to do something about it, unless you want the Society of Wizards to be able to find us with their eyes closed."

Mendanbar looked at her. She was perfectly serious. He set the dishtowel down and drew his sword. It didn't look or feel any different to him from the way it normally felt, but Cimorene winced.

"Can't you . . . tone it down a little?"

"I still don't know what you're talking about," Mendanbar said, irritated. "And even if I did, I wouldn't have the slightest idea how to go about 'toning it down.' "

"Why not? It's your sword, isn't it?"

"It didn't come with directions!"

"Most of them don't." Cimorene shook her head at him and picked another dirty teacup out of the rapidly diminishing stack. "Maybe there's something in Kazul's treasury that will take care of it. I'll check as soon as we're done here."

When the dishes were finished and the kitchen tidied to suit Cimorene's exacting standards, she left Mendanbar to mull things over while she went off to investigate the treasury. Mendanbar was glad of the chance to think.

"What is the Society of Wizards doing?" he muttered. Between the misleading things Zemenar had said to Mendanbar and the downright lies Antorell had told to Cimorene, it was clear that the wizards didn't want them comparing notes. Cimorene might even be right about their desire to start a war between the Enchanted Forest and the dragons.

Starting a war, however, would take more than a misunderstanding between the King of the Enchanted Forest and Kazul's Chief Cook and Librarian. Were the wizards behind the mysterious burned area Mendanbar had found? They could have gotten hold of Woraug's scales, and they certainly could have enchanted them.

"But *why* would they do it?" Mendanbar asked the sink. "They're not stupid, at least Zemenar isn't, and a war would cause the Society almost as many problems as it would cause us. What could make them overlook the problems and try to stir up trouble anyway?" The sink did not answer.

But if it wasn't the wizards, Mendanbar wondered, who was it? Where had Kazul disappeared to? And was there really a dragonsbane farm in the Enchanted Forest, or was that just a rumor someone was spreading to add to the confusion?

He was still trying to put his questions into some sort of order when Cimorene returned. She had exchanged the apron and the rust-colored dress for a dark blue tunic with matching leggings, a pair of tall black boots, and a maroon cloak. She had taken off her crown, and her braids were wound neatly around her head. A gold-handled sword hung at her side, next to a small belt pouch. She held out a sword belt and sheath, the leather gray with age.

"I think this will do the job," she said. "Try it and see."

"I've already got a sheath," Mendanbar pointed out.

"Yes, but this one blocks magic," Cimorene explained. "It'll keep your sword from being so—so obvious all the time. At least, I hope it will."

"If you say so," Mendanbar replied, taking the scabbard. He held it a moment, testing. It didn't feel magical, but then, that was the idea. He shrugged, pulled out his sword, and put it into the sheath Cimorene had given him.

"Oh, that's much better," Cimorene said with evident relief. "I can hardly notice anything now."

"I can," Mendanbar said, touching the hilt with a frown. The pulse of the Enchanted Forest was still there, ready for him to use.

"Of course you can," Cimorene said. "It's your sword."

"Well, I suppose I don't mind using it, then," Mendanbar said. "As long as it doesn't damage the sword."

"It won't," Cimorene promised.

Mendanbar took off his sword belt and set it aside, then buckled on the belt and scabbard Cimorene had given him.

"All right," he said, "let's go."

As they left the cave, Cimorene muttered something under her breath and waved at the entrance. Mendanbar jumped as a coil of strong, hard magic sprang into place behind them. Looking over his shoulder, he saw a solid wall of rock. He transferred his gaze to Cimorene and raised an eyebrow.

"What kind of magic was *that?*"

"Just something Kazul and I worked out a while back," Cimorene said. "It's to keep wizards and knights and so forth from prowling around while I'm gone."

So Cimorene is a sorceress, as well as a cook and librarian and goodness knows what else, Mendanbar thought to himself. Every time he thought he had her figured out, she surprised him again.

"It's a good idea, but please warn me if you're going to do anything like that again," he said. "I'm not in the mood for being startled, if you know what I mean."

Cimorene nodded, frowning slightly, and asked just what it was about the spell that had startled him. This led to a long, technical discussion of the various ways of casting spells, detecting spells, and comparing spells other people had cast. Mendanbar found it both interesting and informative. He had always known that his own methods of working magic were not much like anyone else's, but he had never had time to study other styles. Cimorene knew something about most kinds of magic, and she was naturally very well informed indeed about dragon magic. She was as interested in Mendanbar's system as he was in everything else, and the conversation lasted all the way to Flat Top Mountain.

The sun had slipped behind the mountains and it was almost dark when they came to the foot of the last slope. Mendanbar could see the giant's castle at the top, large and dark and ominous against the graying sky. A broad road wrapped three times around the mountain as it wound its way to the castle gates.

"Are you sure this is the right place?" he asked.

"Quite sure," Cimorene said. "I've never been here myself, but Kazul has described it often enough. And that's certainly a giant's castle."

"Exactly," Mendanbar said. "But is it the right giant?"

"We won't find out standing here. Come on."

Cimorene marched confidently up the mountain. Shaking his head, Mendanbar followed. By the time they reached the castle gates, the stars were beginning to come out and it was getting hard to see.

"There ought to be a bellpull or a knob," Cimorene said. "You check that side of the gate, and I'll take this one."

"All right, but what—"

A loud grinding noise interrupted Mendanbar in midsentence, and the gates swung open. Yellow light spilled across the road, making Mendanbar and Cimorene squint.

"Come in, travelers," a woman's voice said, much too pleasantly. "Come in, and make yourselves comfortable for the night."

Neither Mendanbar nor Cimorene moved. "This was your idea in the first place," Mendanbar said softly to Cimorene. "What do we do now?"

"Ask questions," Cimorene replied just as softly. She raised her voice and said, "Thank you for your kind hospitality, but we're not just traveling. We're looking for the giantess Ballimore, and we're in a hurry. So if you're not Ballimore, we'll have to go on."

"I am Ballimore," said the voice, still in an artificially pleasant tone that made Mendanbar's skin crawl. "Who are you?"

"I'm Princess Cimorene, Chief Cook and Librarian to Kazul, the King of the Dragons, and this is Mendanbar, the King of the Enchanted Forest," Cimorene answered.

"Cimorene?" said the voice in an entirely different manner. "Oh, good. I've been wanting to meet you for the longest time. Come on in, you and your friend, and I'll have supper ready in a jiffy."

Mendanbar and Cimorene looked at each other. "I think it's all right now," Cimorene said after a moment.

"Well, we won't find out standing here," Mendanbar said. He held out his arm. "Shall we go in, Princess?"

Cimorene gave him a bright, almost impish smile, and laid her fingertips on his arm as if they were walking into a court ball. "I should be pleased to accompany you, Your Majesty."

Together they walked through the gate. The courtyard inside was high, wide, and empty except for two rows of blazing torches in iron holders lined up on either side of the path. Mendanbar and Cimorene paced slowly up to the door, which swung open just as the gates had, only without the grinding. As they went in, they heard the castle gates crunch shut. A moment later, the doors closed silently behind them.

They stood in a stone hall three times the size of any Mendanbar had ever seen. A wooden table, surrounded by high-backed chairs, stretched the length of the hall. At the far end of the room a large fire burned in an open hearth. High on the walls, more torches lit the room. A brown-haired woman in a pale blue dress was bending over a cauldron that hung from an iron hook above the fire. It all looked very ordinary, until Mendanbar noticed that the seats of the chairs were level with his eyes and everything else was similarly oversized.

The brown-haired woman sniffed at the cauldron, nodded to herself, and straightened. "Welcome," she said, coming forward. "I'm Ballimore. You must be Princess Cimorene. I'm so pleased to meet you at last, after all that Kazul has told me about you."

The giantess bent over to shake hands gently with Cimorene. She was at least three times as tall as Mendanbar, but she moved with a grace that suited her size. Cimorene returned the handshake gravely, and said, "I hope Kazul hasn't given you the wrong idea about me."

"Not at all, I'm sure," said the giantess. "Is this your young man? You're not running away from the dragons after all this time, are you?"

"Certainly not," Cimorene said with unnecessary vehemence. "I'm very happy with my job."

"Of course," Ballimore said, sounding disappointed. She gave Mendanbar a speculative look, then leaned toward Cimorene. "If I were you, I'd reconsider," she said in a loud whisper. "Your young man doesn't look like the patient type."

"No, no," Cimorene said, reddening. "It's not like that at all. This is the King of the Enchanted Forest,

94

and he came to see Kazul, only Kazul has gone to visit her grandchildren and isn't home. That's why we came to see you—to borrow a magic carpet, so we can find Kazul."

"Oh, I see," said the giantess. "Strictly business. Well, you'll have to wait until after supper. Dobbilan will be home any minute, and he hates it when his meals are late."

"Dobbilan?" Mendanbar said with some misgiving.

"My husband," Ballimore said.

There was a loud crash from the courtyard outside, followed by the *thud*, *thud*, *thud* of heavy footsteps that shook the castle.

Ballimore straightened with a happy smile. "Here he comes now."

8

In Which They Give
Some Good Advice to a Giant

❖

Mendanbar and Cimorene turned to face the castle doors as the footsteps drew nearer. A moment later, the doors flew open and the giantess's husband stepped into the hall. He was a giant's head taller than she, with wild brown hair and a beard like a large, untidy broom's head. He carried a club that was as long as Mendanbar was tall.

Just inside the door, the giant stopped and sniffed the air. Then he sneezed once, scowled ferociously, and said in a voice that shook the torches in their brackets:

"Fee, fie, foe, fum,
I smell the blood of an Englishman.

> Be he alive or be he dead,
> I'll grind his bones to make my bread."

Ballimore shook her head. "Nonsense, dear. It's just Princess Cimorene and the King of the Enchanted Forest."

"And neither of us is English," Cimorene added.

The giant squinted down at her. "Are you sure about that?"

"Positive," Mendanbar said.

"Well—" The giant sniffed again, experimentally, then lowered his club with a sigh. "That's all right, then. I wasn't in the mood for more work tonight, anyway. Sorry about the mistake. It must be this cold in my head."

"I told you yesterday to take something for it," Ballimore scolded. "And I told you this morning to wrap some flannel around your throat before you went out. But do you listen to me? No!"

"I listen," the giant protested uncomfortably. "But I can't ransack villages with a piece of flannel around my neck. It wouldn't look right."

Cimorene snorted softly. Mendanbar got the distinct impression that she didn't think much of doing things for the sake of appearances.

"Well, really, Dobbilan," Ballimore said, "how do you think it looks if you're coughing and sneezing all over everything while you're ransacking? Have a little sense."

"I'd rather have a little dinner," said Dobbilan and sneezed again.

"If you sound like that tomorrow, you're staying home in bed," Ballimore informed her husband.

"I can't do that! I'm scheduled to pillage two villages and maraud half a county."

"You're in no condition to pillage a henhouse, much less a village," Ballimore declared. "Besides, you've earned a bit of a rest, what with all the extra time you've been putting in lately, looting and marauding and I don't know what all."

"That's not the point."

"It's precisely the point. You're just being stubborn because you think having a bad cold is un-giantlike."

"Well, it is."

Ballimore shook her head and looked at Cimorene. "Men!" she said in tones of disgust.

"And don't you say 'men' to me," Dobbilan said. "It's my job we're talking about."

"Maybe you should try a different line of work," Mendanbar suggested.

"Eh?" Dobbilan peered down at him with interest. "Like what?"

"Consulting," Mendanbar said at random, because he hadn't actually thought about it.

"Consulting?"

"You know," said Cimorene. "Giving advice to people. You could teach other giants the best ways of— of ravaging and pillaging and marauding, and you could tell villages the best ways to keep giants away. With all your experience, I'll bet you'd be good at it."

"I never thought of that," Dobbilan said, rubbing his chin.

"I don't know why not," Ballimore said. "It's a

very good idea. And you wouldn't be out in all sorts of weather, catching colds and flu and goodness knows what else."

"Plundering *has* gotten to be an awful lot of work lately," the giant admitted. "It would be a relief to stop. I'm getting too old to tramp through fields."

"I understand consulting pays very well, too," Mendanbar told him.

"I'll do it!" Dobbilan said with sudden decision. "Tomorrow morning, first thing. Thank you for the suggestion. What did you say your names were?"

"If you'd listen once in a while, you wouldn't have to ask me to repeat everything," Ballimore said. "This is Princess Cimorene, the one who's been with Kazul for the last year or so and gave me that marvelous biscuit recipe you like so much. And her young man is the King of the Enchanted Forest, who she's not running away with yet."

Mendanbar choked and shot an apprehensive look at Cimorene. She rolled her eyes and made a face at him but did not say anything, having apparently decided it was a waste of effort to correct the giantess.

"Pleased to meet you, Princess," Dobbilan said solemnly. "Nice to see you, King. What brings you to Flat Top Mountain?"

"They say it's business," Ballimore said before either Cimorene or Mendanbar could answer.

"Then it will have to wait until after dinner," Dobbilan announced. "I never discuss business at dinner. Or with dinner, for that matter." He winked at Cimorene. "Besides, I'm hungry." He sneezed a third time. "Excuse me."

Ballimore began scolding again as Cimorene and Mendanbar nodded politely. Mendanbar was beginning to wonder how long they were going to have to stand next to the table, when Ballimore shooed her husband to a seat at one end and started for the other herself, saying over her shoulder, "Cimorene, dear, you and the King are on the right. Just walk around to the chair; it's all set up."

With some misgiving, Mendanbar escorted Cimorene past Dobbilan's chair toward the seat Ballimore had indicated. As they approached, he saw that the giantess had not been exaggerating. A set of normal-sized wooden steps, equipped with wheels so as to be easily movable, stood next to the giant right-hand chair, and two ordinary chairs were perched side by side on the seat at the top. The combination was, Mendanbar discovered, exactly the right height to reach the table. Apparently, Ballimore was accustomed to having smaller people at dinner, for the plates and glasses were the usual size as well. As long as Mendanbar did not look down, it was easy to pretend he was sitting at an ordinary dinner table.

The food was very good. They started with fresh greens and went on to roast pig with cranberries, mushrooms in wine, and some sort of lumpy vegetable in a thick brown sauce that disguised it completely and tasted marvelous. There was a great deal of everything. Mendanbar supposed this was only to be expected at a giant's table, but Ballimore did not seem to realize that a person who was only a third her size would have a smaller appetite as well. She filled and refilled Mendanbar's plate until he was ready to burst.

Near the end of the meal, Cimorene leaned over and whispered, "Don't take any dessert."

"Why not?" Mendanbar asked.

"Ballimore's using her Cauldron of Plenty," Cimorene said, "and it doesn't do desserts very well. So unless you *like* burned mint custard or sour-cream-and-onion ice cream . . ."

"I see," Mendanbar said quickly. "Then it's a good thing I couldn't eat another bite even if I wanted to."

When dinner was over, Cimorene brought up the question of the magic carpet. Ballimore nodded at once.

"Of course you can borrow a carpet, Cimorene dear. I'll just take a look around and see what we have."

"You won't find much," said her husband, and sneezed loudly. "That last Englishman you let in took most of them. You should have let me find him and grind his bones, like I'm supposed to."

"Nonsense," said Ballimore, frowning at her husband. "We can afford a few cheap magic harps and a coin or two. I keep the good silver and Mother's jewelry in the top cupboard, where they can't reach it. Besides, they're always such nice boys."

"Huh," said Dobbilan. "Beggars and thieves, if you ask me, and boring at that."

"What makes you say that?" Mendanbar asked curiously.

"They always do the same thing—come in, ask for a meal, hide, and then run off with a harp or a bag full of money the minute I fall asleep," Dobbilan said. "And they're always named Jack. *Always*. We've lived in this castle for twenty years, and every three months, regular as clockwork, one of those boys shows up, and there's never been a Tom, Dick, or Harry among 'em. Just Jacks. The English have no imagination."

"About the carpet," Cimorene reminded him.

"Oh, that. Well, the last Jack wasn't musical, and he cleaned us out of magic carpets instead of harps." Dobbilan sneezed again and began to cough.

"Bed for you, dear," Ballimore said firmly and shooed her husband out of the room. She followed him closely, muttering to herself about cough syrup and vaporizers and hot tea with lemon and honey. Mendanbar and Cimorene looked at each other.

"Is there anywhere else we can borrow a carpet?" Mendanbar asked.

"Not that I know of," Cimorene said with a worried frown. "We'll just have to walk. Drat. It'll take days."

"We could go back to the Enchanted Forest and—"

"There," said Ballimore, coming briskly into the room and cutting Mendanbar off in mid-sentence. "He'll be much better in the morning. I'm afraid he's right about the carpets, Cimorene dear, but I'll just have a look around and see if there isn't something stuck off in a corner somewhere. I can't believe we're completely out."

"It's quite all right," Cimorene said. "We'll manage somehow."

"Nonsense, dear," Ballimore said in the same tone she used to her husband. "It will be quite an adventure, seeing what's stuck off in corners and so on. I haven't been in some of the storage rooms in years."

It was clear that nothing they could say would shake her resolve, and after a token protest, they gave in. Ballimore showed them to a pair of comfortably furnished rooms and left them for the night. Mendanbar did not object, even though it was still fairly early. The long walk from the dragon's cave had been very tiring. He lay down on the bed and fell asleep at once.

Breakfast next morning was cinnamon-flavored porridge, milk, and toast with blueberry jam. Mendanbar found it waiting on the high table in the central hall when he left his room to look for his hosts. There was no one else around, but the giant-sized dishes and crumbs at either end of the table showed that Ballimore and Dobbilan had already eaten. Mendanbar climbed the stairs to his seat and began dishing up the porridge. Before he had finished filling his bowl, Cimorene walked into the room, peering around for the giants.

"Good morning," Mendanbar called. "Madame Ballimore and her husband appear to have been and gone, but they've left an excellent breakfast. Would you care to join me?"

"I'd be delighted," Cimorene called back, and climbed the stairs to join him. "I had no idea giants were such early risers," she said as she sat down in the second chair. "Where do you suppose they've gone?"

"Gone?" said Ballimore's voice from the hallway at the end of the room. "Dear, dear, I thought sure I'd left enough porridge for the pair of you, but it won't take a minute to make up some more."

"There's plenty of breakfast," Mendanbar said

quickly. "We were talking about you and Dobbilan."

"But he was supposed to wait for you," Ballimore said, emerging from the hallway. She inspected the room over the top of the large bundle she carried, then shook her head. "Isn't that just like a man? Cimorene dear, I've found just the thing for you. I knew there would be something upstairs, no matter what Dobbilan said. Are you quite certain you have enough porridge?"

"Quite certain," Cimorene said. "What—"

"Ballimore! Ballimore, where's the inkwell?" Dobbilan's voice echoed down the corridor, interrupting Cimorene in mid-sentence. "Where are you? Why can't I find anything around here when I want it?"

"Because you never look in the right place, dear," Ballimore called. "The inkwell is in the kitchen next to the grocery list, where it's been for the past six months, and I'm in the dining room. Which is where you'd be if you'd done what I asked you to, instead of wandering off in all directions."

"I didn't wander off," Dobbilan objected, sticking his head into the room. "I went to get some paper and ink so I could write a letter. Oh, good morning, Princess, King. I didn't see you."

"You were supposed to see them," Ballimore said, exasperated. "You were supposed to be here when— oh, never mind."

"Well, if you're done scolding, could you find me that inkwell?"

Ballimore shook her head, set her bundle down on a chair, and went off to deal with her erring husband. Mendanbar looked at Cimorene, and they both burst out laughing at the same time.

"Oh, dear," said Cimorene when she got her breath back. "I hope they didn't hear."

"Are they always like this?" Mendanbar asked.

"I don't know," Cimorene admitted. "This is the first time I've been here. Kazul has always been the one who comes to talk or borrow things." The thought wiped the smile from her face. "I hope she's safe."

"You'd know if she wasn't," Mendanbar said, hoping he was right. "Being King of the Dragons is a little like being King of the Enchanted Forest; if anything really drastic happens to you, *everybody* knows."

"I suppose so," Cimorene said. "And I know perfectly well that she can take care of herself, but I'll *still* feel a lot better when we find out where she is."

There wasn't much Mendanbar could say to that. They ate in silence for a few minutes and were just finishing up when Ballimore and Dobbilan returned. Dobbilan was carrying several sheets of white paper and a pen made of a feather as long as Mendanbar's arm. Ballimore held an inkwell the size of a sink. The giantess cleared the dishes away from the far end of the table and set the inkwell gently in place, then steered her husband to the chair. When she had him settled, she picked up the bundle she had brought in earlier.

"I'll just take this outside and shake the dust out," she told Cimorene. "You and your young man can come along as soon as you've finished eating. Don't rush."

"How do you spell 'resignation'?" Dobbilan asked, nibbling on the end of his feather pen.

Mendanbar spelled it for him as Ballimore bustled

out the door. He and Cimorene finished their breakfasts with only an occasional interruption from Dobbilan. Leaving the giant mumbling over his letter and chewing on the tattered end of his pen, they went out to see what Ballimore had found.

"There you are," Ballimore said as they came into the courtyard. "I've gotten most of the dust out, and it's ready to go. What do you think?"

She stepped back and Mendanbar got his first good look at the carpet. It was enormous, with a three-foot fringe on all four sides. In places it looked rather worn, and there was a hole the size of a teacup in one corner. The background was a rich cream color, dotted with teddy bears a foot long. Pink teddy bears. Bright pink.

"It's certainly large enough," Mendanbar said at last.

"Are you sure it will fly?" Cimorene asked, looking dubiously at the hole.

"Oh, yes," Ballimore reassured her. "It's the very best quality, but we haven't used it in years because of the pattern." She gestured at the teddy bears. "Dobbilan thought they just didn't look right in a giant's castle."

"I think I agree with him," Mendanbar said under his breath, eyeing the pink teddy bears with dislike. "No wonder that Jack fellow didn't take it."

"As long as it flies, I don't care what it looks like," Cimorene declared. "Thank you so much, Ballimore. I'll make sure you get it back as soon as we're through with it."

"There's no rush," Ballimore said. "It'll just go back in the attic."

"How does it work?" Mendanbar asked.

"I couldn't find the instruction manual, but it's perfectly simple," Ballimore told him. "All magic carpets are the same. You sit in the middle and say, 'Up, up, up and away' to make it take off, and you steer by leaning in the direction you want to go."

"What about stopping?"

Ballimore frowned in concentration. "I believe you're supposed to say 'Whoa,' but 'Cut it out, carpet' works just as well. I'm sorry I can't be more definite. It's been a long time."

"Right." Mendanbar looked at Cimorene. "Are you *sure* you want to do this?"

Cimorene hesitated, then nodded firmly. "We'll manage. If I could think of some other way of getting to the north end of the mountains quickly, I would. Come on." She stepped onto the carpet, and plopped down in the center.

With some misgiving, Mendanbar sat next to her.

"Oh, heavens, I nearly forgot!" Ballimore said suddenly. "Stay right there, Cimorene dear. I'll be back in a flash."

"Now what?" Mendanbar asked as the giantess hurried into the castle.

"Maybe she remembered where the instruction manual is," Cimorene said.

"Somehow I doubt it," Mendanbar said.

A moment later, Ballimore came hurrying out again, carrying a large bag. "I packed you a bit of lunch," she explained, handing Cimorene the package. "Goodness knows what you'll find out there in the mountains."

Cimorene thanked Ballimore again and set the bag between herself and Mendanbar, then said, "All right, carpet: up, up, up and away!"

The carpet shuddered, shifted and rose slowly into the air. Smiling broadly, Cimorene waved at Ballimore, then leaned forward. The carpet shivered again and began to move. It sailed up out of the castle and into the sky over the mountains, gathering speed as it went.

9

*In Which They Discover
the Perils of Borrowed Equipment*

At first, the magic carpet ride was thoroughly enjoyable. The air was crisp and cool, and there was no noise at all except their own voices. The view was amazing, even better than looking down from a mountain. The Mountains of Morning stood in crooked, gray-blue rows below, each crack and boulder outlined in sharp black shadow. Tiny figures moved across the rocks and through the strips of greenery at the bottoms of the mountains: sheep and mountain goats and adventurous knights. Every now and then Mendanbar caught a glimpse of the lush trees of the Enchanted Forest between the peaks.

"Stop craning your neck like that," Cimorene said. "You're confusing the carpet."

"Sorry." Mendanbar sneaked a last look and sighed as the patch of green disappeared behind a rocky slope. How was Willin getting along without him?

"Mendanbar, is your sword slipping?" Cimorene said. "I thought I felt something for a minute there. Is it coming out of that sheath?"

"No," Mendanbar replied, checking it. "It's fine. And I haven't touched it. Are you sure it was the sword?"

"No," Cimorene admitted. "Maybe we flew over something magical and that's what I felt. It's gone now."

"Good," said Mendanbar. "Are you—"

The carpet gave a sudden lurch sideways, then dropped three feet. "Mendanbar!" Cimorene cried. "I told you to stop that!"

"It wasn't me!" Mendanbar protested, trying to find something to hang on to.

"Well, it wasn't *me*, and there's only the two of us up here," Cimorene shouted.

The carpet rippled alarmingly, then resumed its peaceful progress. Cautiously, Mendanbar turned his head to look at Cimorene. Wisps of black hair had come loose from her braids to blow wildly across her face. It made her look particularly lovely, even though she was scowling at him. Mendanbar blinked and pulled his thoughts together.

"I really didn't do anything," he said.

"But—"

The carpet wiggled and began to spin slowly. Mendanbar swallowed hard, wishing he had not eaten quite so much breakfast. He closed his eyes, then opened them again very quickly as the carpet bounced twice, paused, and started spinning twice as fast in the opposite direction.

"Carpet!" Mendanbar shouted. "Cut it out!"

The lurching and spinning stopped. The carpet hung motionless in midair for a long moment, then dropped like the bottom falling out of a cardboard box. Cimorene gasped, then said something that sounded like "Oof!" as the carpet froze once more, three feet lower than it had been. Mendanbar started to push himself up, then—without warning—the carpet dropped another three feet.

This time, Mendanbar stayed flat on the teddy bears. Two seconds later, the carpet dropped again. And again. And again. Mendanbar lost track of the bumps and concentrated on keeping track of his stomach. Suddenly, the carpet spun around twice and took off in a steep, fast climb.

"Whoa!" Cimorene cried. "Whoa, you stupid carpet, cut it out!"

Again, the carpet froze. Then it dropped again, but this time, instead of bumping, it fell like a stone. Mendanbar got a glimpse of the ground drawing quickly closer, and then he had both hands on the hilt of his sword. He didn't bother to pull it out of the sheath, he just yanked at the power it held and flung it around himself and Cimorene. Then he shoved with all his might.

Their speed slowed abruptly. The carpet fell away beneath them, rippling angrily, and plopped down on a rocky depression at the foot of a mountain. Mendanbar and Cimorene drifted after it, landing softly in the carpet's center. They lay there for a moment, catching their breath and collecting their wits.

Finally, Mendanbar raised his head and looked warily around. They lay in the middle of a circle of pine trees. "I think we've arrived," he said, sitting up.

"Good," Cimorene said shakily. She sat up, pushing tendrils of hair out of her face, and gave him a crooked smile. "I guess I should have asked Ballimore a few more questions about this carpet before we took it."

"Yes, well, it's too late now." Mendanbar rolled off the carpet and stood up. "How far have we come?"

"A little over halfway, I think. Too far to walk back, not far enough to walk the rest of the way there." She made a face at the teddy bears, which looked innocently back. "We may have to try the carpet again."

"We don't have to try it right away, though," Mendanbar pointed out. "There's a house over there—you can see the roof through the trees. Maybe the owner can tell us exactly where we are and the shortest way to get where we're going."

"All right," Cimorene agreed, with a swiftness that made Mendanbar think she was no more eager to get back on the carpet than he was. "We'll have to bring the carpet with us, though. If you leave magical things lying around, all sorts of dreadful things can happen."

Mendanbar had to admit that she was right, though he wasn't happy about it. They set Ballimore's lunch in the middle of the carpet, then rolled the rug around it, folding the fringe carefully to the inside. Then Cimorene took the front end and Mendanbar picked up the rear, and they started toward the house.

Weaving through three rows of pine trees, they ducked under the low-hanging branches along the outer edge of the grove and emerged in front of the house. It looked, thought Mendanbar, as if it had been put together by the same person who had built his palace, except that instead of too many towers and staircases, this house had too many windows: square windows, round windows, wide windows, tall windows, skinny windows, diamond windows, tiny windows filled with milky glass, enormous picture windows, windows with stained glass pictures of ladies in sweeping robes and birds with gold feathers, open windows with curtains blowing out of them. The roof was made of red tile and skylights, and the chimney had a square block of clear glass in the front side. Even the door had a window in it, right in the middle at about waist height. With only two floors, there were hardly enough walls to hold all the windows, in spite of the way the building sprawled in all directions.

As they drew near, Mendanbar felt a faint aura of power around the house, hanging in the air like mist. He was about to mention it to Cimorene, when he heard yells and shouts of laughter coming from behind the house. Suddenly a small blonde girl dashed around the corner and stopped short, staring. A slightly larger boy followed in hot pursuit and barely managed to stop in time to avoid a collision. The blonde child looked at him reproachfully, then turned toward the house and shrieked at the top of her voice, "Herman! Herman, there's people."

"Bah!" A deep, cross voice came carrying through the open window beside the door. "I don't want any people. Tell them to go away."

The little girl obediently turned to Cimorene. "Go away, please," she said, and stuck her thumb in her mouth.

"No, thank you," Cimorene responded. "We want to talk to your parents."

"Haven't got any," said the boy. He tilted his head to one side, as if considering, then took off for the house at a dead run. "Herman, they won't go!" he shouted as he ran. "They want *parents*. They—"

His shouting stopped as he dove headfirst through the open window and vanished inside. One of the upstairs windows scraped open, and two older children poked their heads out. At the same time, three small heads appeared at the corner of the house, gazing timidly at Mendanbar and Cimorene.

Cimorene looked at Mendanbar and set her end of the carpet on the ground. Mendanbar put his end down, too, and stepped forward to stand beside her. The children stared at them without speaking.

"ABSOLUTELY NOT!" the cross voice shouted. The front door of the house flew open and a dwarf stomped out. He was not much taller than the oldest of the children, but his long black beard and muscular arms showed plainly that he was no child. His hair looked like an upside-down black haystack. He glared angrily at Mendanbar.

"I won't do it!" the dwarf declared before either Mendanbar or Cimorene could say anything. "I don't care if it's family tradition, I don't care if you need the money, I don't care if her mother lied and now you have to convince your council, I don't care if your mother is going to turn her into a toad tomorrow if she doesn't perform. I WILL NOT DO IT AND THAT'S FINAL!"

"That's quite all right," Cimorene said. "We don't want you to. We just want—"

"I know what you want," the dwarf said, hopping furiously from one foot to the other. "You want a chance to talk me into it. Well, you won't get one, missy. You should be ashamed to even consider such a thing!"

"She *isn't* considering it," Mendanbar said. "We're travelers, and we've just stopped to get some directions."

The dwarf paused in midhop. Balancing on one foot, he peered suspiciously at Mendanbar. One of the children giggled. The dwarf glared in the direction of the sound, then turned back to Mendanbar.

"Directions? What sort of directions?" he asked with evident mistrust. "Who are you, anyway?"

"I'm Princess Cimorene and this is King Mendanbar," Cimorene said, "and we're trying to get to the cave where the dragon Falgorn lives."

"Oh, you're after a dramatic rescue," the dwarf said with relief. "I suppose that's all right. But are you sure you know what you're getting into? Dragons are tough."

"No, no," Cimorene said in the exasperated tone of someone who is very tired of correcting the same mistake over and over. "I'm Chief Cook and Librarian for Kazul, the King of the Dragons, and I'm very happy with my job, and I don't want anyone to rescue me."

The dwarf's eyes narrowed. "Then why are you looking for this other dragon?"

"Because I have an urgent message for Kazul, and she's gone to visit Falgorn," Mendanbar explained.

"Huh." The dwarf hesitated, looking from Cimorene to Mendanbar. "How do I know this isn't some sort of trick?"

"Why should we want to trick you?" Cimorene asked.

"To get me to spin straw into gold for you, you silly girl," the dwarf said. "That's why everyone comes to see me. And look at the thanks I get: children! Hundreds and hundreds of children! Bah!"

The littlest children giggled and pulled their heads back behind the corner as the dwarf spun around. The blonde girl stared solemnly at him for a moment, then took her thumb out of her mouth, ran forward, and gave the dwarf an enormous hug.

"Thank you, Herman," she told the dumbfounded dwarf. She hugged him again and skipped off, apparently tired of listening.

The dwarf smiled foolishly after her. The expression made him look pleasant and almost handsome. After a moment, the dwarf turned back to Cimorene, and his frown returned.

"I don't see the connection between children and spinning straw into gold," Mendanbar said before the dwarf could start complaining again. "Would you be good enough to explain it to me?"

"Explain?" the dwarf fumed. "That's what the last

girl said, and what happened? Twins, that's what happened! And *she* claimed she couldn't remember which one was first, so I ended up with both of them."

"I can see why that would be annoying," Cimorene said noncommittally.

The dwarf glared at her. "Yes, you say that *now*, but—oh, what's the use? You'll get it out of me one way or another."

"If you'd rather not tell us—," Mendanbar started, but the dwarf cut him off with a despairing wave.

"It doesn't matter. It's my fate, that's what it is. I should never have agreed to learn to spin straw into gold in the first place."

"Why did you?" Mendanbar asked.

"It's a family tradition," the dwarf answered gloomily. "Of course it doesn't work if you're just spinning for yourself. So, a long time ago, my great-grandfather offered to use his talent to help out a girl who was in a sticky situation. If he hadn't been such a do-gooder, I wouldn't be in this mess."

"What good did he do, exactly?" Mendanbar asked.

"The local prince had gotten a notion that the girl could spin straw into gold," the dwarf said. "Brainless young idiot, but they're all like that. If she could spin straw into gold, why was she living in a hovel? Anyway, Gramps said he'd do her spinning for her in return for part of the gold and her firstborn child. She agreed, but naturally when the baby was born she didn't want to give him up. So Gramps agreed to a guessing game: if she could guess his name, she could keep the baby.

Then he let her find out what his name was. She kept the baby and Gramps kept the gold, and everyone went home happy."

"I think I'm beginning to get the idea," Cimorene said. "It's not just spinning straw into gold that's a family tradition, is it? It's the whole scheme."

The dwarf nodded sadly. "Right the first time. Only I can never make it work properly. I can find plenty of girls who're supposed to spin straw into gold, and most of them suggest the guessing game, but I've never had even *one* who managed to guess my name."

"Oh, dear," said Cimorene.

"I even changed my name legally, so it would be easier," the dwarf said sadly. "Herman isn't a difficult name to remember, is it? But no, the silly chits can't do it. So I end up with the baby as well as the gold, and babies eat and cry and need clothes, and the gold runs out, and I have to find another girl to spin gold for, and it happens all over again, and I end up with *another* baby. It isn't fair!"

"You, um, seem to be fond of the children, though," Mendanbar said.

The dwarf looked around to see whether any of the children were within hearing distance, then nodded sheepishly. "They're good kids. It's just that there are too many of them. I moved out here so it would be harder for the silly girls to find me and talk me into spinning for them, but they keep finding me anyway."

"It was a rather drastic move, wasn't it?" Cimorene said. "What about the dragons and giants and rock snakes and so on?"

"Oh, they're no problem. The house used to belong to a magician, and he left a lot of guarding spells on it. Nothing nasty can get anywhere near."

"*That's* why it feels magical," Mendanbar said, relieved.

"It's an odd sort of house for a wizard," Cimorene said, studying it. "Why so many windows?"

"Not a wizard," the dwarf said. "A magician. He was trying to find out which kinds of windows work best when they're enchanted."

"Did he find out?"

"I suppose so, or he wouldn't have let me buy it. Most of the windows don't work anymore, but there's a round one at the end of the attic that still shows things once in a while."

"What kinds of things?" Mendanbar asked. "Can you ask to see something in particular, or does it just show scenes at random?"

"You have to ask," said the dwarf, "and you don't always get an answer. Would you like to see it?"

"Yes, please," Cimorene said quickly.

Mendanbar looked doubtfully at the carpet, wondering whether it would be safe to leave it where it was with all the children around, and thinking how much trouble it would be to haul along if they didn't.

"Let it be," the dwarf said, following Mendanbar's gaze. "The kids won't touch it."

With some reluctance, Mendanbar nodded and followed the dwarf and Cimorene into the house. The inside was just as mazelike as Mendanbar had expected from the rambling exterior. The dwarf led them down a passage, around a corner, up a flight of creaky wooden stairs, through a room lined with pictures, up another flight of stairs, and down a long hall to a cramped, stuffy little room under the farthest slope of the roof. The only light came from a circular window about twice the size of Mendanbar's head.

"There it is," said the dwarf. "If you want to see something, ask; but I can't guarantee it'll work."

"Show me Kazul, the King of the Dragons," Cimorene commanded at once.

For a moment, nothing happened. Then Mendanbar felt a tentative swelling of magic around the window. "I think it needs a boost," he said and reached for his sword.

"No, let me," said Cimorene. She thought for a minute, then raised her right hand and pointed at the window.

> *"Power of water, wind, and earth,*
> *Cast the spell to show its birth.*
> *Raise the fire to stop the harm*
> *By the power of this charm."*

Power surged around the window, and the glass went milk-white. "What did you do?" Mendanbar said, impressed.

"It's a dragon spell," Cimorene told him, keeping her eyes fixed on the window. "It's easy to remember, and it's not hard to adapt it to do just about anything. I found it in Kazul's—look!"

The window glass had cleared. Through the circular pane, Mendanbar could see the inside of a large cave. A sphere of golden light, like a giant glowing soap-bubble, covered half the cave, and inside the glow was a dragon. She was easily four times as tall as Mendanbar, even without counting her wings. Three short, stubby horns stuck out of her head, one on each side and one in the center of her forehead, and her scales were just starting to turn gray around the edges. An angry-looking trickle of smoke leaked out of her mouth as she breathed. In front of the bubble stood two tall, bearded men in long robes, carrying staffs of polished wood.

"Wizards," Cimorene said angrily. "I knew it!"

10

In Which Mendanbar
Decides to Experiment

Mendanbar stared at the window, angrier than he could remember being in a long time. In the back of his mind, he could hear a voice reminding him that the King of the Dragons was no concern of the King of the Enchanted Forest and that the Society of Wizards was a dangerous group to offend or interfere with. He could hear another voice that sounded very like Willin's, suggesting envoys and formal complaints. But he was in no mood to pay attention to either of them. Mendanbar was not going to stand by and let the Society of Wizards kidnap and imprison anyone, King of the Dragons or not.

"Huh," said the dwarf. "So you weren't kidding about looking for that dragon."

"Of course not," Cimorene snapped. Her eyes were fixed on the window, and there was a little crease between her eyebrows. "But where are they? Window! Show me where they are."

Magic rose up around the window in a great wave, and Mendanbar felt an answering surge in his sword. The window turned bright green, glowing brighter and brighter, then suddenly shattered into dust.

"Hey!" said the dwarf. "My window!"

"Drat!" Cimorene's hands clenched into fists, and she glared at the empty space where the window had been. After a moment, she shook her head and turned to the dwarf. "I'm sorry, Herman. I didn't know it would do that. And we don't really know any more than we did before."

"Oh, yes, we do," Mendanbar said. "We know that some wizards have captured Kazul, and we know that they're somewhere in the Enchanted Forest."

"We do?"

"I'm sure of it. I think that's why the window couldn't show a more general picture of where they were. Things in the Enchanted Forest move around a lot, especially if the forest doesn't like something. I'll bet my best crown that that"—Mendanbar waved at the empty window frame—"is something the Enchanted Forest doesn't like one bit."

"All right, but that doesn't help much," Cimorene said. "The Enchanted Forest is a big place. How are we going to find them?"

"That won't be a problem," Mendanbar said. "I'm the King of the Enchanted Forest, remember?"

"That makes you good at finding missing dragons?"

"It makes me good at finding out what's going on," Mendanbar said. "I can tell when places are moving around, and I can get where I want to go even when it's moving. I don't think it will be too hard, once we get back inside the forest."

"Then let's go," Cimorene said. "I didn't like the look of that bubble thing those wizards had around Kazul."

"At least they don't seem to have hurt her," Mendanbar offered.

"That's true. Oh, I *wish* I knew what they were up to!" Cimorene scowled at the broken window, then turned sharply away, almost running into the dwarf.

"I don't understand this at all," the dwarf said, looking from Cimorene to Mendanbar with a puzzled frown.

"I'm sorry we don't have time to explain," Mendanbar said. "But I'm afraid we don't."

"Thank you for all your help," Cimorene added.

The dwarf shook his head and led them back to the front door, frowning in such deep concentration the whole time that neither Mendanbar nor Cimorene could bring themselves to interrupt. In the doorway, the dwarf paused.

"Are you *sure* you don't want any gold?" he asked.

"Quite sure," Mendanbar said. "We have a long walk ahead of us, and gold is awfully heavy."

"I thought you didn't want to spin gold anymore," Cimorene added.

The dwarf looked down. "It's not the spinning, it's the rest of it," he said, not very clearly. "And spinning's the only way I know to make money, and you wouldn't believe how fast kids grow."

"Oh," said Cimorene. She bit her lip. "What if we asked you to spin some gold for us and then let you keep it?" she asked without much hope.

"No," said the dwarf. "I tried it once. It just doesn't work."

"Can you spin for the children?" Mendanbar asked.

The dwarf shook his head. "They're my responsibility, so it's the same as spinning for myself as far as the spell is concerned."

"What *are* you going to do with them all?" Cimorene asked as renewed shrieks and the sound of pounding feet came through the open door.

"Oh, most of them will grow up and save their kingdoms from something or other in the nick of time," the dwarf said. "Long-lost heirs, you know. That's what makes it so difficult. I have to see that they're properly trained on top of everything else."

"Training," Mendanbar said under his breath. He squinted into the sunlight, trying to catch hold of an idea that hovered just out of reach.

"I don't suppose their parents . . ." Cimorene's voice trailed off as the dwarf shook his head.

"A bargain's a bargain. Besides, it wouldn't be the same without them running all over. I *can't* give them back."

"Of course not," Mendanbar said, blinking. He smiled suddenly. "But you *can* charge for training them, can't you?"

An answering smile lit up Cimorene's face. "A boarding school for long-lost heirs. What a good idea!"

"A school?" the dwarf said as if the words tasted funny. "A boarding school? I don't know—"

"Why not?" Cimorene said. "It would solve your money problems for sure. Special schools are always horribly expensive. You could charge the parents of your children for just the training part, and take on a few more kids at training plus full room and board."

The dwarf's eyes gleamed at the idea, but then his face fell. "What about my spinning?" he said. "It *is* a family tradition."

Cimorene rolled her eyes. "Haven't you done enough of that already?"

"Well—"

"I have an idea about that, too," Mendanbar put in. "The problem with the spell is that you can't spin for yourself or for anyone who's your responsibility, right?"

"That's it in a nutshell," the dwarf said. "And there's nothing to be done about it."

"What if you set up a scholarship fund?" Mendanbar said. "I'll bet a really good lawyer could design one that would get around the spell's restrictions so you could spin for it."

Cimorene nodded. "A good lawyer can get around just about anything. And if that doesn't work, you could spin for other scholarship funds and only take part of the gold, the way you usually do."

"I never thought of spinning for a fund," the dwarf said in wonder.

"You think about it, then," Mendanbar said. "We have to go."

"Yes," said Cimorene. "I won't feel quite comfortable until I know Kazul is out of that bubble. Thank you again."

They left the dwarf in the doorway, muttering to himself about rooms and expenses, and walked over to the rolled-up carpet.

Mendanbar looked at it with distaste, remembering their wild ride. He hoped Cimorene wasn't going to insist on using it right away. His stomach hadn't completely settled from the last time. He turned his head. Cimorene was looking at him with a wary expression.

"Let's carry it for a while," she suggested. "The children are probably watching, and we shouldn't give them ideas."

"Right," Mendanbar said with relief. "Do you want the front end or the back?"

Cimorene took the back end, and they hoisted the carpet to their shoulders and started off. Walking with the carpet was surprisingly easy. Cimorene was a good match for Mendanbar in height, and she was quite strong. Mendanbar supposed it must be from carrying around dragon-sized servings of lamb and beef, and before he thought, he said as much.

"Actually, it's the chocolate mousse and cherries jubilee," Cimorene said.

"I didn't think chocolate mousse was particularly heavy."

"It is when you've got a bucket full of it in each hand," Cimorene retorted.

"Oh," said Mendanbar. "Yes, I suppose it would be."

He was trying to figure out how much a bucket of mousse would weigh when the carpet jerked suddenly. Mendanbar grabbed at it, thinking *Oh, no, it's going to start dancing around on its own!* Then he realized that the carpet had jerked because Cimorene had stopped. He looked reproachfully over his shoulder.

"It's time for lunch," Cimorene said. "All this talk about food is making me hungry, and I don't want to have to face a lot of wizards on an empty stomach."

Now that she mentioned it, he was hungry, too. "Good idea," Mendanbar said with enthusiasm. "And this looks like a nice spot to stop. Will you serve, or shall I?"

Cimorene laughed. They set the rolled-up carpet on a stretch of grass between two pines and got out Ballimore's package, then sat down to see what the giantess had sent along with them. It was, as Mendanbar had expected, an enormous quantity of food—seven fat pastries stuffed with chicken and herbs, a large bottle of cold spring water, a round loaf of bread and a generous wedge of yellow cheese, four large red apples, and a small box filled with a wonderful, creamy chocolate fudge.

"My goodness," Cimorene said when they had unpacked everything. "Ballimore certainly believes in feeding people well. *Look* at all of this!"

"No, no," Mendanbar said, picking up one of the

pastries and handing it to Cimorene. "Don't look at it. Eat it."

"I wonder where she got the fudge," Cimorene mused. "Everything else is probably from the Cauldron of Plenty, but it doesn't do desserts very well."

"Maybe she made it herself."

"I hope so." Cimorene smiled at Mendanbar's look of surprise. "If she did, I can ask her for the recipe."

By an unspoken mutual agreement, neither Mendanbar nor Cimorene mentioned Kazul or the wizards during lunch, though they were both certainly thinking about them. Instead, they had a pleasant talk about some of the odd and interesting people they had each met over the past few years. Cimorene knew a lot of unusual folk. Many of them were dragons, of course, but her position as Kazul's Chief Cook and Librarian meant that she had also met most of the visitors from outside the Mountains of Morning who came to pay their respects to the King of the Dragons or to ask her questions.

Near the end of the meal, Mendanbar noticed that Cimorene was gazing intently at him. No, not at him: at his sword.

"What is it?" Mendanbar asked worriedly.

"Have you been doing things with that sword again?" Cimorene demanded.

"No," Mendanbar said, puzzled. "I used it on your sink, and to stop the nightshade, and when the carpet started falling, but that's all. Why?"

"Because it's leaking magic all over the place," Cimorene said. "I thought so before, but now I'm positive." She finished her second pastry and stood up, brushing crumbs from her lap. "That sheath must not be as good as I thought. Would you mind letting me look at it? Without the sword."

"Not at all," Mendanbar answered. He stood up and drew the sword. Cimorene flinched. "Is something wrong?"

"I don't know," Cimorene said. "Can't you feel it?"

"Feel what?"

"Your sword. It isn't the sheath after all; it's that dratted sword. It's gotten worse. Put it away, quickly."

Thoroughly puzzled, Mendanbar did as Cimorene asked. "All right," he said. "Now, would you please explain?"

"I'm not sure I can," Cimorene said. "You didn't know what I meant before, when I said your sword reeked of magic, so I suppose it's reasonable that you can't tell that the reek is twice as strong now. You'll just have to take my word for it."

Mendanbar looked down at the sword, thinking hard. "It's linked to the Enchanted Forest, and I've never taken it out of the woods before," he said at last. "Maybe it doesn't like it. Maybe it's trying to make the mountains more like the Enchanted Forest." It sounded silly put that way, but he couldn't think how else to say it. It would sound even sillier if he told her that he thought the sword was trying to stuff some magic into the empty, barren-feeling land around it.

"Um," said Cimorene, gazing absently at the sword. After a moment, she looked up. "I'll bet you're right. Bother. That means we *have* to use the carpet."

She bent and started packing up the remains of their lunch.

"Wait a minute," Mendanbar said. "What has my sword got to do with that carpet?"

"If being *outside* the Enchanted Forest is what makes your sword behave like a—a magic beacon, then we have to get it back *inside* the Enchanted Forest as fast as we can," Cimorene explained patiently. "Otherwise every ogre and wizard for leagues and leagues around will come looking for whatever is making all the fuss. And the carpet is a lot faster than walking."

"I don't trust it."

"We managed before. It ought to be easier now that we know what to expect. Here, help me." She knelt and began unrolling the carpet as she spoke.

"*Do* we know what to expect?" Remembering the bumping, spinning, unpredictable ride, Mendanbar shuddered.

"Look, I don't like it any better than you do, but we have to do *something* about that sword. Besides, the sooner we get to the forest, the sooner you can find out where those wizards have Kazul. And do we have any other choice?"

"I could probably use the sword to get us to the Enchanted Forest," Mendanbar suggested.

Cimorene sat back on her heels, staring at him. "You can do that? Why on earth didn't you say so to begin with? We could have gone straight to Kazul's grandchildren's cave and saved a lot of time."

"I didn't mention it before because I'm not *really* sure it will work," Mendanbar said. "I've never tried that particular spell outside the Enchanted Forest before, and it wouldn't be a good idea to test it for the first time to get somewhere I've never been. Especially somewhere that isn't in the Enchanted Forest either."

Actually, he hadn't tried *any* of his usual spells outside the Enchanted Forest before, for the very good reason that he hadn't *been* outside the Enchanted Forest since he'd become King and started working magic, but he didn't like to mention that in front of Cimorene. He was quite sure that if *she* had suddenly become the ruler of a magical kingdom, she would have tested all her new spells and powers and abilities immediately, under as many different conditions as she could come up with. He didn't want her to think he was careless or neglectful.

"So we can either experiment with the carpet again or experiment with your spell," Cimorene said. She scowled thoughtfully at the teddy bears, then looked up at Mendanbar and smiled. "Let's try the spell. What do you want me to do?"

"Just stand there," Mendanbar said, returning her smile. "I've never worked with another magician, and one experiment at a time is enough."

"Why haven't you?" Cimorene asked as she climbed to her feet. "Worked with another magician, I mean. From what you were telling me yesterday, you've got more than enough work for a couple of assistants."

"I've never had time to find any assistants," Mendanbar said. "Except Willin, my steward, and he's never learned much magic."

"You mean you're trying to run the whole Enchanted Forest *by yourself?*" Cimorene said. "You're as bad as the dragons!"

"What?"

"It took me six months to persuade them that the King of the Dragons didn't need to do everything all the time," Cimorene explained. "And then it took me three more months to get a system set up so they wouldn't keep running to Kazul with every little problem."

"You set up a system? How? I mean, how did you know . . ." Mendanbar's voice trailed off.

To his surprise, Cimorene flushed very slightly. "I studied a lot of unusual things when I was growing up," she said. "Unusual for a princess, I mean. Politics was one of them."

"It sounds like a perfectly reasonable thing for a princess to study to me," Mendanbar said. "Look how useful it's been for you."

"Well, it's not one of the things a princess is *supposed* to learn," Cimorene said. "You wouldn't believe the fuss they made when they found out I'd talked my protocol teacher into covering it."

"What were you supposed to be learning, then?"

Cimorene made a face. "Embroidery and dancing and etiquette and *proper* behavior."

"No wonder princesses are silly, if that's all they're supposed to know about," Mendanbar said without thinking. He blinked and added hastily, "Not you. I mean, you aren't silly, even if you are a princess. I mean—"

"Don't try to explain any more; you'll only make

it worse," Cimorene said, laughing. "Now, hadn't we better try that spell? We *are* in a bit of a hurry, remember."

"Right." With some difficulty, Mendanbar pushed the discussion out of his mind and tried to remember how he had been planning to work the transportation spell. Usually he simply twisted one of the threads of power that crisscrossed the Enchanted Forest, pulling himself to his destination, but outside the forest there were no threads that he could feel. There was power in the sword, though, and it was linked with the Enchanted Forest. If he pulled on that, he should be able to move whatever he chose back to the forest.

Before he moved anything, however, he would have to indicate who and what he wanted to move. He didn't want to arrive in the Enchanted Forest with a magic carpet covered with pink teddy bears and no Cimorene. Mendanbar suppressed a sigh. Spells were so much easier at home, where he didn't have to think about them as much. He dismissed that thought and concentrated on figuring out the shape of the spell he wanted.

When he was satisfied that he knew exactly what he intended to do, and in what order, he put a hand on the hilt of his sword and looked at Cimorene. "Ready?"

"Whenever you are," Cimorene said.

Mendanbar nodded and drew his sword. He heard Cimorene suck in her breath as he raised the weapon over his head and swung it in a slow circle. Carefully, he pointed the sword at the carpet and pushed a tiny bit of power out to label it for the next part of the spell.

Then he pointed the sword at Cimorene and repeated the process even more gently than before. Cimorene shivered, but she remained silent.

Turning, Mendanbar pointed the sword in the direction of the Enchanted Forest. Now for the tricky part. He drew on the power in the sword, feeling it hum through the hilt and into his hands. In his mind he pictured the giant trees of the Enchanted Forest, ranged in silent rows around the rocks that edged the Green Glass Pool, with the still water reflecting them like a green mirror. When he was sure he had the picture clear and steady in his mind, he gave the power in the sword the same twisting pull he used to move from place to place within the Enchanted Forest.

Slowly, almost reluctantly, the rocks began to blur and fade. Mist rose, wavering, to veil the mountains and sky. Then, just as the landscape was about to vanish into thick, woolly grayness, the mist stopped condensing. For a moment, everything was still. Then the mist thinned and the outlines of the rocks and mountains grew sharper.

Almost, thought Mendanbar. *It must need more power because we're outside the Enchanted Forest.* He clenched his hands around the hilt of the sword and pulled again, hard.

Gray fog slammed down around him like a window shutter dropping closed. Something hit him like a giant's hammer, and he felt himself falling. *Now I've done it*, he thought vaguely, just before everything went black. *I hope Cimorene is all right.* Then he lost consciousness completely. He didn't even feel himself land.

11

*In Which Mendanbar
and Cimorene Are Very Busy*

Something was wrong. Mendanbar could feel it, even before he was fully awake. The magic of the Enchanted Forest floated all around him, but it seemed tenuous and tottery, almost disconnected. He thought he had better get up and fix it. He opened his eyes.

Cimorene's concerned face hovered a foot above him. Her braids had come loose from their tight crown and there was a worry line between her eyebrows. He didn't want her to be worried. He tried to say so, but all he managed was a coughing fit. Cimorene bit her lip, and her troubled expression intensified.

"Don't try to talk," she said unhappily. "Don't try to do anything yet. Your sword is safe, and I'm all right, and everything else can wait for a few minutes. Just lie there and breathe slowly."

It occurred to Mendanbar that Cimorene was anxious about *him*. That was nice, in a way, but he still didn't want her to be unhappy. In fact, it was suddenly very important to him that Cimorene should not be worried or unhappy in the slightest. He closed his eyes to consider how best to convey this and fell asleep at once.

When he woke, the sky was the pale blue of late afternoon. Rubbing his eyes, he sat up carefully, remembering what had happened earlier when he'd tried to talk. Cimorene was at his side at once.

"Are you sure you should do that?" she said.

"It hasn't hurt so far," Mendanbar replied. "What happened?"

Cimorene studied him for a moment, then relaxed visibly. "I'm not sure," she said. "One minute we were going somewhere, and the next minute we weren't. When I picked myself up, you were lying there looking three-quarters dead and as white as cracked ice, and you've been that way for over four hours. If that's your transportation spell, I think I would have preferred the carpet."

"At least it got us to the forest."

"Not exactly."

Mendanbar blinked at her, then looked around. The carpet, on which he and Cimorene were sitting, lay in the center of a twenty-foot circle of thin green fuzz. Seven saplings, pencil-thick and none more than waist high, poked randomly upward through the fuzz. Beyond the circle, patches of short, brownish-green grass alternated with mottled gray rock that rose quickly into cliffs and ridges and the sudden, sharp heights of mountains that shadowed them all. None of it looked familiar, though it still felt vaguely like the Enchanted Forest to him.

"Well, at least we went *somewhere*," Mendanbar said after a moment.

"Yes, but where? Those are the Mountains of Morning, but this bit"—Cimorene waved at the green fuzz and the saplings—"looks as if it belongs in the Enchanted Forest. So what's it doing here?"

"It feels like the Enchanted Forest, too," Mendanbar said. He shifted, and his hand touched cool metal. Even without looking, he knew it was his sword. He picked it up and looked at it thoughtfully. "Cimorene, is this still 'leaking magic' the way you said it was earlier?"

"No," Cimorene said. "I can tell it's a magic sword, and an odd one at that, but only if I study it. It's not— not so *obvious* anymore."

Mendanbar pushed himself to his feet. It took more effort than he had expected, and by the time he finished, the worry line had reappeared between Cimorene's eyebrows.

"I'm all right," he told her. "Mostly." He waited a moment for his head to stop spinning, then walked cautiously to the edge of the circle of fuzz. He stepped over the boundary onto a patch of grass. The comforting sense of being surrounded by magic vanished, and although he had more than half expected it, he staggered slightly.

Cimorene was beside him almost at once. "What is it?"

"It was just the change. Can you feel my sword now?"

"Yes," Cimorene said. "But it's nowhere near as bad as it was this morning."

"I was afraid you were going to say that." Mendanbar looked at the circular area of green and sighed. "I hate to do this, but you're right. It doesn't belong here."

He started forward. Cimorene grabbed his arm. "Wait a minute! What are you talking about?"

"This." Mendanbar pointed at the saplings with his sword. "In a way, it really *is* part of the Enchanted Forest. That's why it feels like home to me, and that's why the sword doesn't feel 'obvious' when it's inside."

"That makes sense," Cimorene said. She still had hold of his arm. "But how did it get here?"

"I don't think it did, exactly," Mendanbar said. "I think the sword made it for us when we couldn't get through to the real forest. That's why it's so—so new-looking."

"Your sword . . ." Cimorene paused, thinking. "Yes, you told me it was linked to the Enchanted Forest." She looked at the green area. "I didn't realize it could do things on its own, without someone directing it."

"Normally it doesn't," Mendanbar said. "Unless it's picking the next King of the Enchanted Forest."

"Picking the next . . ." Cimorene's voice trailed off and she shook her head. "I think you'd better tell me about that sword. All about it, not just dribbles of information when something comes up. I have a feeling we're going to need to know."

"I don't know that much," Mendanbar said. "And I have to take care of these things first." He waved at the saplings.

"What are you going to do?"

"If the sword did it, it ought to be able to undo it," Mendanbar said. "I don't want to erase this patch, but I can't think of anything else to do with it. It wouldn't be a good idea to leave a bit of my kingdom disconnected like this."

"No, I can see that," Cimorene said, releasing his arm at last. "Just watch what you're doing with that spell. It's going to be dark soon, and I don't want to spend another four hours waiting for you to wake up."

"I don't like the idea myself," Mendanbar said. "Don't worry. I'll be careful."

"You'd better be."

Mendanbar smiled, raised the sword, and walked back into the tiny forest. He paced around the edge, getting the feel of the magic that was spread spiderweb thin across the circle. Then he stopped. With his left hand, he lowered his sword so that the tip rested on the green fuzz that might one day have grown into moss. With his right, he reached out and touched the web, gathering in the threads. When his hand was full, he began to feed the threads into the sword.

It was touchy work, for the invisible strands were thin and fragile, and he knew that if he missed even one he would have to begin all over again. The task took a lot of concentration, for the sword accepted the threads with great reluctance. He was not at all sure he would have the strength to do it twice, so he worked with painstaking slowness.

When he was halfway through, the saplings began to shrink. Slowly at first, then faster and faster, the little trees grew shorter and more slender, until they disappeared into the green fuzz. For a moment, nothing more seemed to happen. Then the circle of green began to shrink. Like a drop of water being sucked up by a napkin, the green edge drew back toward the sword, leaving bare rock behind. In a moment, the retreating border was out of sight beneath the carpet.

Mendanbar continued feeding magic into the sword. There were only a few threads left, and he slowed down even more. A puddle the size of a wagon wheel was all that was left of the original circle. It shrank to the size of a dinner plate, then a pancake, then a penny. Then it was gone.

For a heartbeat longer, Mendanbar held his position, checking to be certain he had not missed anything. Finally he let go of the end of the spell and lifted the point of the sword from the ground. He felt much better than he had when he began. He looked up and smiled at Cimorene.

"That was extremely interesting," Cimorene said. She eyed the bare ground around the carpet. "Is that all of it?"

"I think so. Why?"

"Because if we don't want to spend the night here, we're going to have to leave quickly. It'll be getting dark soon." Cimorene paused, then added, "You'd better put that sword away. It's dripping magic again."

"Sorry," Mendanbar said. "Why don't we—"

With a rattle of small stones and a vicious hiss, a long, gray-black snake shot out of a crevice at the top of the nearest cliff and dropped toward Cimorene. Mendanbar jerked his sword up and sent a crackling bolt of power to meet the serpent. The hiss became a choking gurgle as the snake flared into a bright line of fire and disintegrated. Flakes of ash drifted the last few feet to fall around Mendanbar and Cimorene.

Three more snakes launched themselves from parts of the cliff, and another slithered from behind a boulder. From the corner of his eye, Mendanbar saw Cimorene yank her sword out of its sheath. He hoped briefly and intensely that she was good at fighting, and then he had no time or attention for anything except the snakes.

A second blast of magic disposed of two of the three in the air, and a single sword-stroke chopped the third in half. By then four new snakes were in the air, and Mendanbar could hear more hissing on all sides. He sent another spell skyward, and another, then swung at two snakes that had leaped from a crack barely shoulder-high above the ground. After that he lost track of how many snakes he struck or stabbed or chopped and how many he burned or blasted. He had no time for anything but fighting. He swung his sword until his arms were tired and his head hurt from concentration and spell-casting. And then, suddenly, there were no more snakes.

The ground was dusted with ashes and littered with pieces of snakes, and the air smelled of charred meat. Slowly, Mendanbar lowered his sword. A few paces away, Cimorene was straightening up from a fighter's crouch with the same wary hesitation. Her sword was covered with dark blood, and there were quite a lot of dead snakes around her.

"Oh, wonderful," Mendanbar said with heartfelt sincerity. "I was hoping you were good with a sword."

"You aren't bad with one yourself," Cimorene replied a little breathlessly.

"It's a magic sword," Mendanbar reminded her, but he felt absurdly pleased nonetheless.

Cimorene grinned. "So is mine. I know a little about fencing, but not enough to do me any good against most of the things in the Mountains of Morning. That's why Kazul lets me carry this." She lifted her sword, and a drop of snake blood fell from the tip. She frowned and began fishing in her pockets with her free hand. "It's supposed to make the bearer impossible to defeat."

"Sounds good to me," Mendanbar said, looking at the bits of snake near Cimorene's feet. "What's the catch?"

"Getting killed isn't the same as being defeated," Cimorene said. She pulled a handkerchief from a pocket, smiled, and began cleaning the sword with it. "Not always, anyway. And it doesn't keep you from getting hurt, either. So I still have to be careful. Do you want to use this?" She held out the stained handkerchief.

"Thank you," Mendanbar said, taking the square of cloth. He wiped his sword carefully, resheathed it, and hesitated. "Do you want it back? I'm afraid it's ruined."

"That's all right," Cimorene said. "I always carry one or two extras." She retrieved the handkerchief, grimaced, and tied it into a tight bundle, which she stowed in her belt pouch. "There. Now, let's get out of here."

"Why such a hurry?"

"We still have to rescue Kazul. And besides—do you *want* to fight more rock snakes?" Cimorene asked. "That's what we'll be doing if we stay. We've cleaned out this part pretty well, but there's sure to be several other colonies around." She pointed at a dark ridge a couple of hundred feet farther on. "There, for instance. Or there." She gestured in the opposite direction, at a wrinkled cliff.

"I don't see how we can get past them on foot," Mendanbar said, frowning.

"Well, we can't stay here. They'll slither over as soon as the last of the light goes. We'll have to take the carpet."

"I wouldn't recommend it," said a new voice.

Together, Mendanbar and Cimorene turned. The voice belonged to a dark-haired man who stood calmly next to the magic carpet, watching them with interest. He was several inches shorter than Mendanbar, with bright blue eyes and a neatly trimmed beard and mustache. He wore tall black boots, dark gray leggings, a loose-sleeved, high-necked shirt in pale gray, and an open knee-length black vest covered with pockets of all shapes and sizes. Under the vest, his wide black belt was hung with strangely shaped pouches and sheaths. The air around him crackled with magic.

"Who are you?" Cimorene asked. "And why don't you want us to use the carpet?"

"My name is Telemain," said the man, bowing, "and I have a considerable familiarity with the basic mechanics of carpets. Magic ones, that is. And this carpet"—he gestured left-handed, and three silver rings glinted in the fading light—"is plainly defective."

"Defective?" Mendanbar said suspiciously. Telemain didn't *look* like a wizard, but that didn't necessarily mean much. Wizards could wear disguises as well as anyone else.

"Oh, it will probably operate, after a fashion," Telemain said. "But not well, and not for long. I'm surprised you got this far on it."

"We didn't, exactly," Mendanbar said. "And we *have* had some trouble with it. What do you suggest?"

The sound of a pebble bouncing down a series of rocks echoed along the narrow canyon. "I suggest we talk somewhere else," Telemain said, glancing toward the sound. "This isn't a safe place, even with my defensive enchantments fully erected."

"And how do you suggest we get there?" Cimorene asked.

"Like this." Telemain raised a hand and made a circle in the air with his forefinger. As he did, he muttered something, then clapped both hands together.

The canyon flowed and melted into a sloping meadow halfway up a mountainside. "Much better," Telemain said. "No rock snakes, trolls, ogres, or other dangerous wildlife. I guarantee it."

Mendanbar was inclined to believe him. Trolls and ogres liked places where they could jump out from behind things or pop out from under rocks. An open meadow didn't have enough cover. Besides, Telemain was no longer surrounded by the hum of magic, which meant he had dropped his guarding spell.

"Now," Telemain went on, "how *did* the two of you get into a ravine full of rock snakes with a defective magic carpet? Having rescued you, I think I am entitled to some explanation."

"We were on our way to the Enchanted Forest," Cimorene said carefully, pushing wisps of loose hair out of her face. Mendanbar noticed with approval that she said nothing about their reasons for wanting to go there. "How did you happen to come by at such a convenient moment?"

"I was—looking for some people I thought might be in this area," Telemain said. "By the way, what are your names?"

"This is Cimorene and I'm Mendanbar," Mendanbar said. "Who were you looking for?"

"You, I think," Telemain said, smiling. "That is, if you're the same Cimorene and Mendanbar who visited Herman the dwarf earlier today."

"That was us," Cimorene said cautiously.

"Good! Then I can settle this quickly and get back to my work. How did you—"

"Excuse me," Mendanbar interrupted. "But how do you know Herman? And how did you find us?"

"I know Herman because he bought his house from me," Telemain said. He was beginning to sound irritated. "I also maintain certain defensive enchantments, which are especially designed to prevent incursions by noxious creatures, around the house and neighboring areas for him. When someone demolished the scrying spell I had established on the attic window, I felt obliged to investigate. Herman was in the middle of an explanation about visitors and dragons when I sensed an extremely interesting sorcerous flare to the northwest."

"I knew that dratted sword was going to get us in trouble," Cimorene muttered.

"Before I had time to locate it precisely, there was another burst of magic, which I recognized as a transportation spell," Telemain continued. He frowned disapprovingly. "A rather confused one. It has taken me all afternoon to disentangle the traces and discover your whereabouts. Does that satisfy you?"

"I think so," Mendanbar said. "I'm sorry if we seem overly mistrustful, but we've already had some trouble with one wizard and we've reason to expect more. So you see . . ."

"I am *not* a wizard," Telemain said emphatically. "I'm a magician. Can't you tell?"

"No," Cimorene said. "What's the difference?"

"A magician knows many types of magic," Telemain said. "Wizards only know one, and they're very secretive about it. I've been researching them for years, trying to duplicate their methodology, but I still haven't managed a workable simulation."

"What?" said Cimorene, looking puzzled.

"He's been trying to figure out how the wizards work their spells," Mendanbar explained, "but he hasn't done it yet."

"Why do you want to know that?" Cimorene asked Telemain with renewed suspicion.

"Because that's what I do!" Telemain said. "I just told you that. And if you'll answer a few questions for me, I can go back to doing it. How did you shatter that window?"

"We asked it to show us something," Mendanbar said. "It couldn't, so it broke."

Telemain shook his head. "Impossible! That particular glass was enchanted to reveal anything, anywhere, even in the Enchanted Forest. If it couldn't discover the object of your inquiry, the viewing plane would display an empty information buffer."

"What does he mean?" Cimorene asked, frowning.

"He means that if the window couldn't find what we were asking about, it should have just stayed blank," Mendanbar explained.

"That's what I said." Telemain nodded emphatically. "It should *not* have broken."

"Well, it did," Cimorene told him. "And we don't have time to stand around arguing. We have to get to the Enchanted Forest and rescue a friend of mine. So could you just tell us what's wrong with our carpet?"

"Nonsense," Telemain muttered. "You *must* have done more than frame a question." He intercepted a look from Cimorene and sighed. "Oh, very well, I'll examine the carpet. Spread it out so I can see all of it at once."

They unrolled the carpet the rest of the way. Telemain's eyebrows rose in surprise at the sight of the teddy bears, but he did not comment, for which Mendanbar was grateful. When the carpet was stretched full-length on the meadow, Telemain paced twice around it, frowning and gesturing occasionally. Then he turned to Mendanbar and Cimorene and shook his head.

"The landing compensator has a gap in it, and the flight regulator has completely deteriorated," he said. "It needs more than I can do without special tools and yarn for reweaving. You'll have to take it to a repair shop."

"Wonderful," Cimorene said sarcastically. "This *would* happen with a borrowed carpet."

"Can you recommend a good place?" Mendanbar asked Telemain. "Preferably somewhere close," he added, noting the pink tint of the sky to the west. The sun would be completely down in another hour, and he didn't want to wander around the Mountains of Morning in the dark.

"Or can you send us straight to the Enchanted Forest?" Cimorene asked. "We're in kind of a hurry."

"The Enchanted Forest requires a complex and destination-specific enhancement to the basic transportation spell module," Telemain explained. "But the repair shop is simple."

He raised his left hand and made the same circular gesture he had before. "Gypsy Jack's," he said, and clapped, and the meadow and the mountain melted and flowed. The mountain bulged higher, and the meadow flattened and grew rockier. A long, rectangular section of ground squeezed upward and settled into the shape of a narrow house on wheels.

"There," Telemain said with great satisfaction. "We've arrived."

12

*In Which Yet Another Wizard
Tries to Cause Trouble*

They were standing in front of the wheeled house. At least, Mendanbar assumed it was the front because there was a door at the end of the long side facing them. Two iron steps, black and worn with age, led up to the door. The house itself was painted a cheerful blue with yellow shutters and a yellow trim around the door. There were four windows on the side facing Mendanbar, lined up in a neat row next to the door like chicks following a hen. The roof above the windows was low but not quite flat, and covered with wooden shingles that looked brand-new. There were four pairs of wheels, too, the rims painted blue to match the house and the spokes painted yellow to match the shutters.

A beautifully lettered sign on a stick had been pounded into the ground next to the door: "Ask About Our Low Prices!"

Mendanbar looked at Cimorene. Cimorene looked from Mendanbar to the wheeled house to Telemain.

"Don't do that again without asking first," she said to the magician.

"I thought you'd be pleased," Telemain said. "Look at all the time you've saved."

"Asking doesn't take much time."

"Where are we, exactly?" Mendanbar put in before they could start arguing. "And what is that?" He pointed at the house on wheels.

"That is Gypsy Jack's home," Telemain answered. "If anyone can mend that carpet of yours, he can. As to where we are, all I can tell you is that we are still somewhere in the Mountains of Morning. If you want a more precise location, you will have to ask Jack. Assuming he remembers; he moves around a lot."

"How did you find him, then?" Cimorene asked.

"Oh, Jack supplies me with unusual things now and then, when I need them for a spell or an experiment," Telemain said. "I pay him by enchanting his house for him. Any good magician can find his own spells."

"Enchanting his house?" Mendanbar said. "You mean, to keep ogres and things from bothering it, the way you did Herman's?"

Telemain shook his head. "I offered, but Jack wasn't interested. He has his own way of discouraging unpleasant company. No, what he wanted was a spell to keep the paint from fading."

"Why does he need you to put spells on his house?" Cimorene asked.

"Jack isn't a magician," Telemain said. "He does a little bit of everything—smithing, gardening, music, tailoring, pretty much any trade you can think of. For example, he designed and built his house. He has a rare knack for patching up a spell that's wearing thin, but he can't set up a complex enchantment on his own. That's why he deals with me."

One of the windows scraped open and a head poked out. "Yo! You going to stand there all night and maybe get eaten by a dragon? Not that I would dream of interfering with your plans, but if a quick exit is what you want, I got a dozen faster ways, all very cheap."

"Hello, Jack," Telemain called. "I've brought you some customers."

"Customers! Why didn't you say so? I'll be right out." The head vanished and the window screeched closed.

"Customers?" Cimorene said, looking at Telemain.

"You want that carpet fixed, don't you? Jack can—"

The door of the house flew open with a bang, and a large man leaped over the steps and landed in front of them. He had a thick black mustache, long black hair, bright black eyes, and a wide white grin. Pushing a soft, baggy cap back from his forehead, he bowed deeply.

"Welcome to my home, friends of Telemain!" he boomed. "And very welcome you are. What's the problem?"

"A little difficulty about transportation, Jack," Telemain said before Mendanbar or Cimorene had quite recovered from the man's abrupt appearance. "We were hoping you could help."

"No trouble! What do you need? Shoes? I got a barrel full—sandals, clogs, dancing shoes, walking shoes, horse shoes . . ." His voice trailed off and he looked hopefully at Telemain.

"Nothing that simple," Telemain said. "The difficulty is magical in nature."

"Ah! You want seven-league boots! Well, you're in luck. A pair of 'em just came in this morning. They're practically brand-new, hardly been used at all. Or there's a swell pair of ruby slippers that'd be perfect for the lady. I'll throw in the magic belt that goes with 'em for free. Or—"

"No, no, Jack," Telemain interrupted. "The problem is with this." He stepped aside and let Jack get a good look at the magic carpet.

Jack's eyes narrowed to slits of concentration. He stepped forward and studied the carpet, then paced around it, much as Telemain had done earlier. "No kidding," he said at last. "That carpet's a problem, all right."

"Can you fix it?" Cimorene asked.

"Sure. Give me a week, and she'll be good as new."

"A week!" Cimorene looked at him in dismay. "Can't you fix it any faster than that?"

Jack spread his hands out and shrugged. "Maybe, but I can't promise. It depends on how fast I can get parts."

"Then we'll leave it here and go on without it tomorrow," Mendanbar said. At least they wouldn't have to carry the thing around anymore, and they wouldn't be tempted to use it in spite of its hazards. "You can send it home when it's finished, can't you?"

"Shouldn't be a problem." Jack smiled. "Where do you want it?"

Cimorene hesitated. "You're not one of those Jacks who go around killing giants, are you?"

"Lady, what do you think I am, stupid or something?" Jack asked. "I'm a businessman. I don't *do* giants."

"Then please send the carpet to Ballimore the Giantess on Flat Top Mountain when you're done fixing it," Cimorene said. "And the bill to Cimorene, Chief Cook and Librarian, in care of the King of the Dragons."

"King of the Dragons, eh?" Jack said thoughtfully.

"Yes, and don't go padding the bill, Jack," Telemain warned.

"Me? Wouldn't dream of it." Jack kicked the carpet into a loose roll and heaved it up onto his shoulder. "Anything else?"

"Is there a safe place near here where we can spend the night?" Mendanbar asked.

"Sure," Jack said. He balanced the carpet with one hand and jerked the thumb of the other at the blue-and-yellow house on wheels. "Right there. I got two spare rooms on the end I can rent you for as long as you want 'em."

"Tonight is all we need," Mendanbar said, and Cimorene nodded.

Jack bobbed his head in a way that managed to suggest a full-fledged formal bow, then started toward the house, carrying the carpet. Mendanbar turned to Telemain. "Thank you very much for your help."

"You're welcome," Telemain said, and started after Jack.

"Hey!" Cimorene said. "Where are you going?"

"To arrange for my own bed and board," Telemain explained patiently. "You didn't really expect me to leave before you'd answered my questions, did you?"

Without waiting for a reply, the magician followed Jack into the house. Mendanbar and Cimorene looked at each other, shrugged, and went in after them.

The front door of Jack's house opened into a cluttered room painted a bright green that clashed with almost everything. Fortunately, most of the walls were hidden behind piles of boxes, barrels, bales, and bundles. Jack propped the carpet in a crowded corner, where it leaned precariously against two paintings balanced on a stack of books. Then he set about fixing dinner.

Cimorene kept Telemain's attention occupied while Jack worked, and at first Mendanbar was glad of it. He wanted time to think and to sort out some of the confusing things that had happened in the last two days. He was sure that a few of them were important, and if he could only concentrate for a little while he could figure out which ones.

He quickly discovered that it was not going to work. The conversation between Cimorene and Telemain was much too distracting, even though he was not particularly interested in anything they were talking about. Finally he gave up trying to think and listened instead.

"—window wasn't up to it," Cimorene was saying. "So I used a spell to boost it."

"And that broke it?" Telemain said, frowning.

"No," Cimorene replied. "It worked just fine. The window turned white, and then showed Kazul and a lot of wizards." Her face darkened. "And when I catch up with them—"

"Yes, of course," Telemain said hastily. "What happened next?"

"I told the window to show me where they were, and *then* it broke."

"I can fix up a new one for you," Jack put in over his shoulder. "I got some glass around somewhere, and it's no trick at all to cut it to size."

"I'll think about it, Jack," Telemain said. He looked at Cimorene. "The window just . . . broke? It didn't show anything at all?"

Cimorene nodded. "Not a thing. Right, Mendanbar?"

"Right," Mendanbar said. "The picture of Kazul and the wizards disappeared, and the window turned bright green, and then it broke. I think it was trying to show us a place inside the Enchanted Forest and couldn't."

"It should have been able to," Telemain said. "I tested it very thoroughly. I suppose the enchantment might have been wearing thin. What kind of spell did you say you used to boost it?" he asked, turning to Cimorene.

Cimorene hesitated, then shrugged. "It was a dragon spell I found in Kazul's library last year. It's very adaptable, and—"

A shout from outside the house interrupted Cimorene in mid-sentence. "You in there! Come out at once. There's no point in hiding."

Jack muttered something and stuck his head out the window. "Hang on!" he shouted. "I'll just be a min—"

Something exploded outside, knocking Jack back through the window and making the whole house rock. "Come out!" the voice repeated. "Now!"

"Wizards got no patience," Jack muttered, glaring at the window.

Mendanbar stiffened and looked at Cimorene.

"We'd better go out, or he'll tear the house down," she said. "Jack, can you mix up a bucket of soapy water with a little lemon juice in it, quick?"

"Huh?" said Jack.

"A bucket of soap and water and lemon juice," Cimorene repeated impatiently. "It melts wizards. Hurry up and bring it out after us. I think we're going to need it."

"Soapy water with lemon melts wizards?" Telemain said with great interest. "How did you discover that?"

Another explosion rocked the house. "Never mind that now," Cimorene said. "Come on!" She pushed the door open and darted out.

With a muttered curse, Mendanbar followed. He remembered the steps just in time to jump over them instead of tripping. As he landed, he dodged to one side and pulled his sword out. Only then did he stop to look around.

Cimorene stood with her back against the house,

watching the wizard warily. The wizard was very easy to see, even though it was by now quite dark, because he was glowing as brightly as a bonfire. He was taller than the wizard who had invaded Cimorene's cave, and he wore red robes instead of blue and brown, but his staff was of the same dark, polished wood and his sandy beard was just as long and scraggly. Mendanbar wondered irrelevantly whether the Society of Wizards had a rule against its members trimming their beards.

"Cimorene!" the wizard said. "I might have guessed. What have you—no, you *haven't* got it. Where is it?"

"Where is what?" Mendanbar demanded. "And what do you mean by causing all this commotion? Didn't anyone ever teach you to knock on doors and ask for things politely?"

"So you've picked up a hero," the wizard said to Cimorene with a sneer. "He won't do you any good. Where is it?"

"I don't know what you're talking about," Cimorene said.

"Neither does he," Telemain commented from the doorway. "Unless he's even more fuzzy-headed than he seems. From the way he's been leaping to conclusions without any evidence at all, that's entirely possible."

The wizard's eyes narrowed and he pointed his staff at Telemain. "Who are you?"

"That's the first intelligent thing you've said since you arrived," Telemain said. "My name is Telemain. I'm a magician."

"A magician!" The wizard sucked in his breath. "I

suppose we are after the same thing. I warn you, you had better not cross me. I represent the Society of Wizards in this matter."

"*What* matter?" Cimorene asked crossly.

"Yes, you have displayed a lamentable lack of precision in your account of your purposes," Telemain said. "Just what—"

Mendanbar felt the harsh swell of the wizard's magic an instant before the spell left the man's staff. Without thought, he swung his sword to parry it. As it touched the bolt of magic, the sword hummed hungrily. A shiver ran up Mendanbar's arm from the hilt of the sword to his shoulder, and the spell was gone.

"I wouldn't do that again, if I were you," Mendanbar told the wizard.

Everyone stared at Mendanbar. The wizard was the first to recover. "The sword!" he cried. "I should have seen it at once. Excellent! This makes everything easy."

He moved the end of his staff a few inches to point at Mendanbar and muttered something under his breath. Mendanbar sensed magic building up in the staff again. This time he didn't wait for the wizard to release the spell. He pushed a tendril of his own magic out through the sword and touched the wizard's staff gently with it.

Power flowed into the sword like water being soaked up by a sponge. The feeling of magic that surrounded the wizard vanished, and so did his glow. The wizard gave a squawk of surprise. He lowered his staff, staring at Mendanbar.

"How did you do that?" he demanded. "You're

just a hero. How could you possibly reverse my spell?"

"I didn't reverse your spell," Mendanbar said. "I stopped it, that's all. And I'm *not* a hero. I'm the King of the Enchanted Forest."

The wizard's eyes widened. Certain that the man was going to try another spell, Mendanbar reached out with the sword's magic, hoping to stop him before he could properly begin. He wasn't quite fast enough. As the threads of the sword's magic wrapped themselves around the wizard's staff, the wizard disappeared.

There was a moment of silence. "Mendanbar, what did you *do*?" Cimorene said at last.

"Nothing," Mendanbar said. "I wasn't quick enough. I'm sorry. I should have expected him to try to get away."

Telemain walked over to the spot where the wizard had been standing. "Interesting," he muttered. "Very interesting—ah!" He bent over, and when he straightened up he was holding the wizard's staff in one hand.

"Here's your bucket," Jack said from the door of the house. "What's all this about wizards?"

"It doesn't matter now," Cimorene said. "He's gone."

"Then you won't be needing this?" Jack said, lifting the bucket.

"Don't throw it out," Mendanbar said hastily. "We might want it later. In case he comes back."

"I seriously doubt that it is necessary to worry about his return," Telemain said as he rejoined them. "Wizards depend a good deal upon their staffs. Without his, our recent visitor is unlikely to be much of a problem." He sounded very satisfied with himself, and his fingers stroked the staff lightly as he spoke.

"Then he's sure to come back for it," Cimorene pointed out.

"Yes, but how long will it take him to get here?" Telemain responded. "I assure you, he didn't transport himself anywhere close by. We'll be long gone by the time he makes his way back."

"*We?*" said Mendanbar.

"Of course." Telemain smiled. "I've been trying to get my hands on one of these"—he lifted the wizard's staff—"for years. You've managed to get hold of one in a few seconds. You don't think I'm going to miss an opportunity like this, do you?"

"If that's all you want, keep it," Mendanbar said. "I haven't any use for a wizard's staff."

"Neither have I," Cimorene agreed.

Telemain bowed. "Thank you both." He paused. "I would still like to join you, if you are willing. There are other matters I find intriguing about you."

Completely at sea, Mendanbar stared at the magician.

Cimorene sighed. "Mendanbar, your sword is at it again, worse than ever. I'll bet that's what he means."

"Oh." Mendanbar put his sword back in its sheath and inspected Telemain for a moment. The magician was still something of a puzzle, but he had been very helpful so far. And it was clear from the wizard's behavior that magicians and wizards did not get along, which was another point in Telemain's favor. "I can't promise I'll let you study my sword, but it's all right with me if you come along." He glanced at Cimorene.

"It's fine with me, too," Cimorene said. "But you'd better hear the whole story before you make up your mind. You might not want to come with us after all."

"If you're all done out here, come in and eat," Jack said. "Supper's ready, and if you're sure there won't be any more wizards, I'll just use this water for the dishes afterward."

13

*In Which They Return to
the Enchanted Forest at Last*

*T*hey told Telemain and Jack the whole story over dinner and discussed it late into the night. Telemain was intrigued by their description of Kazul's imprisonment.

"You say these wizards have an enchantment capable of confining a dragon?" he said eagerly. "Are you sure?"

"That's certainly what it looked like," Cimorene said, pouring herself a cup of hot chocolate. The stew and the dinner dishes had long since been cleared away and were piled in the bucket of soapy water waiting for someone to have the time or the inclination to wash them.

Mendanbar wondered idly whether a bucket of

soapy water plus lemon juice plus dishes would be as good for melting a wizard as one without dishes, and what effect the dishes would have on the process. Being melted was probably not very comfortable, but being melted while cups and plates and forks were falling on your head was likely to be even less so.

"I knew I was right to join you," Telemain said, smiling. "I might not have heard about this enchantment at all, if I hadn't. It sounds like a simple modulation of the upper frequencies of a standard reptilian restraint spell, but on an enormously increased scale. I wonder where they're getting the power."

"I don't care how they did it," Cimorene snapped. "I care about getting Kazul *out* of it as soon as possible."

"A trivial detail, once the construction of the spell is properly understood," Telemain said confidently.

"Trivial?" Mendanbar said. "Aren't you forgetting about the wizards? I don't think they'll just let us walk in and take their spell apart."

"And goodness knows what they'll do to Kazul in the meantime," Cimorene muttered.

"Nonsense," Telemain said. "I comprehend your concern, but it is highly unlikely that this episode will prove more than a minor inconvenience so far as your dragon friend is concerned."

Cimorene did not look convinced, so Telemain launched into a lecture on the political implications of the situation, the main point of which was that it would be stupid for the Society of Wizards to hurt Kazul and that wizards were not stupid. Privately, Mendanbar thought that it had been stupid of the wizards to kidnap

Kazul in the first place, but saying so would not re-assure Cimorene, so he kept quiet.

After a while, Telemain finished his lecture. He did not wait for Cimorene to respond, but turned at once to Mendanbar and asked about his sword. Like Cimorene, the magician could feel the sword spilling magic "like a beacon on a mountaintop," and he was amazed—and completely fascinated—to learn that Mendanbar noticed nothing unusual.

"I don't understand why I didn't spot it at once," Telemain said, shaking his head over his cup of chocolate (which looked to Mendanbar as if it had gone cold during his long speech about the relative intelligence of wizards).

"You mean when you met us?" Cimorene said. "Mendanbar's sword wasn't spraying magic all over right then. He'd just used up most of it on the rock snakes."

"It seems to recover very quickly," Telemain said with a sidelong look at the sword. "Is it always like this?"

"How should I know?" Mendanbar said, running a hand through his hair in frustration. "I can't tell when it's doing it, much less when it isn't."

"Yes, you said that before." Telemain sipped at his chocolate, staring absently into space. "I shall have to think about this for a while," he said at last, as though making a profound announcement. "It's a pity you haven't time to visit my tower for a few tests—"

"Absolutely not!" Mendanbar interrupted.

"We have to rescue Kazul from the wizards," Cimorene put in quickly. "Before this business turns into more than a *minor inconvenience*. Before those wizards decide she's too much trouble to keep around and feed her some dragonsbane."

Telemain considered this for a moment. "An excellent idea," he said at last with evident sincerity.

Mendanbar and Cimorene stared at him.

"If the Society of Wizards poisons the King of the Dragons, there is certain to be a war," Telemain explained. "Wars are very distracting. I don't like being distracted; it interferes with my work. So it would be a very good thing if we made sure there was no war."

"I'm so glad you think so," Cimorene said. Her voice sounded a little strange.

The discussion continued for a little longer, but it was getting late and everyone was tired. Finally, Jack suggested that they go to bed.

"It's all very well for you adventurous types to sit around jawing until past midnight, but *some* people have work to do in the morning," he said pointedly.

"I am not an 'adventurous type,' " Telemain said with dignity. "I am in research."

"Fine, fine," Jack said. "So go research my second-best bed. You and the King, here, take the room on the right, Princess Cimorene gets the one on the left, and I get to bunk under the kitchen. Good night, everybody."

That settled things for the evening, but the conference continued the next morning over a breakfast of flapjacks and honey.

"It seems very likely to me that you are correct about Kazul's location," Telemain said. "She is probably being held somewhere in the Enchanted Forest. Our first task, therefore, must be to find her."

"Our first task is to get back into the Enchanted Forest," Mendanbar corrected. "I don't even know which direction it's in anymore."

"It's over that way," Jack said, waving at the large mountain in back of the house. "Not far if you're flying, but a long way to walk. You have to go around, you see. Now, I've got a nice broomstick that'll get you there in a jiffy. It's extra long, so it'll seat all three of you very comfortably, and it's hardly been used at all."

"No, thank you, Jack," Telemain said firmly. "Broomsticks are only reliable transportation for witches. We will manage this ourselves. Pass the flapjacks, please."

"Here," said Cimorene, handing him the plate. "Do you mean that you're going to take us to the Enchanted Forest the same way you brought us here? I thought it would be harder than that."

"Actually, it is," Telemain said. "The Enchanted Forest is unique, magically speaking, and therefore the interface between the forest and the rest of the world is equally unique. Penetrating that interface requires a specific application."

"What's that mean, when it's at home?" said Jack.

"You need a special spell to get into the Enchanted Forest, because it's different from everywhere else," Mendanbar translated.

Telemain looked irritated. "That's what I just said."

"Is that why Mendanbar's spell dropped us into the ravine with the rock snakes instead of in the forest?" Cimorene asked.

"Possibly." Telemain frowned. "It seems unlikely, however. Mendanbar's magic is of the same variety as that of the forest. It should have worked perfectly well, assuming it worked at all."

"Well, why didn't it?" Mendanbar asked crossly. He was getting tired of puzzles, especially puzzles connected with *his* sword, *his* magic, and *his* forest.

"I'm afraid I can't answer that from your description," Telemain replied, his frown deepening. "I can think of half a dozen things that might have gone wrong, but without seeing it myself I don't know which of them it was."

"So do it again, and watch it this time," Jack said. "Hand me the honey, would you, Your Majesty?"

Mendanbar picked up the honey pot, which was shaped like a fat purple bear. Resisting the urge to throw it at Jack's head, he handed it over and said mildly, "I don't think I like the idea of repeating the spell. Last time it knocked me out for four hours, and I'm not willing to do that again just so Telemain can find out why."

"Oh, that's easy enough to fix," Telemain said. "A few wards, properly set, and there won't be any backlash worth worrying about."

"How much backlash does it take before you worry about it?" Cimorene asked, sounding dubious about the whole idea.

"A three-day headache," Jack put in before Telemain could answer. "And that's only because if his head hurts he has trouble thinking about the wherefore of the whatsit."

"That is a serious exaggeration," Telemain said stiffly. "And I don't anticipate that this experiment would result in any kind of prolonged effect, particularly if I set wards first. I have some idea of what to expect, you see, so I can customize the shielding spells to correspond to the specific variety of backlash."

"It sounds good," Cimorene said. "I think. But what happens if it doesn't work?"

Telemain began a long, involved, and somewhat indignant explanation of why his shielding spells could not fail to work. Mendanbar listened with only part of his mind; the rest was busy thinking about Telemain's suggestion. It looked to him as if the only way they were likely to get back into the Enchanted Forest was by means of his own magic. Telemain hadn't actually said he couldn't do it himself, but Mendanbar was fairly sure that was what he had meant. And from the way Jack talked, walking would take more time than they had to spare.

Even if it took Telemain two tries, or three, to figure out what had gone wrong with Mendanbar's transportation spell, it would still be much faster than walking. Of course, they could always rent some of Jack's wares, but after their experiences with the magic carpet, Mendanbar was not at all happy with that idea.

Repeating the spell would be a chance to find out more about the sword, too. His adventures since leaving the Enchanted Forest had made Mendanbar see just how little he really knew about his magic, and the sword seemed like a good place to start finding things out. The only question was, could the wards actually keep the transportation spell from knocking him head over heels again?

"Telemain, how sure of these shielding spells are you?" Mendanbar asked as soon as there was a lull in the conversation.

Telemain looked at him. "Very sure indeed. I have just spent no little time and breath telling Princess Cimorene, here, exactly how sure that is, why I am sure, and how unlikely it is that I am wrong. Obviously, you have not been attending. Do you wish me to repeat the entire explanation?"

"No, of course not," Mendanbar said hastily. "I'm sorry I wasn't listening, but I had to think for a minute."

"And?" said Cimorene.

"And I think we should do it. As long as Telemain is *sure* he can keep me from being knocked out again, that is."

"I am," Telemain said, sounding faintly put out. "I have been telling you that all morning."

"Good," said Jack. "I like to have things settled. You sure you don't want a pair of seven-league boots for backup?"

"There are three of us and you only have one pair of boots," Cimorene pointed out.

They finished breakfast quickly and helped Jack clear up. Telemain had some things to discuss with Jack, so Mendanbar and Cimorene went outside to give them a chance to talk alone. Mendanbar noticed that the worry line between Cimorene's eyebrows was back.

"What's the matter?" he asked.

"Are you sure about this?" Cimorene said. "Doing the transportation spell, I mean. After what happened before . . ."

"I'll be more careful this time," Mendanbar said. "And Telemain's wards should help. Between the two of us, it ought to be all right."

Cimorene did not look convinced. "You're still taking a big chance. There are other ways to get into the Enchanted Forest."

"Not in a hurry, there aren't," Mendanbar said. "And once we get back, we still have to find Kazul. We can't afford to waste any more time."

"I know." Cimorene chewed on her lower lip, frowning. "Look, you're the King of the Enchanted Forest. You shouldn't be taking chances like this just to help me out."

"I *like* helping you out," Mendanbar said. "But it's not just that. It's my job to take care of the Enchanted Forest. If the wizards have Kazul trapped somewhere in my kingdom, it's *my* responsibility."

"You're not responsible for what the Society of Wizards does!"

"No, but when it involves the forest it involves me, too, and I have to try to put it straight."

"No wonder you looked so tired when you showed up at Kazul's cave," Cimorene muttered. "Mendanbar—"

The door of the house slammed. Telemain came hurrying down the steps, carrying the wizard's staff "I'm sorry I kept you waiting," the magician said. "Are you ready to start?"

"Yes," said Mendanbar.

"You aren't bringing *that* along, are you?" Cimorene demanded, eying the staff with disfavor.

"Of course I'm bringing it along," Telemain said. "I told you how long I've been looking for one. If I leave it with Jack, odds are he'll sell it to somebody before the day is out. He wouldn't be able to help it. Here, hold this for a minute while I set up the wards."

With visible reluctance, Cimorene took the wizard's staff. She grimaced as her fingers touched it, as if it felt slimy and unpleasant. At the same time, Mendanbar laid a hand on his sword and pushed a tendril of magic at the staff, to see whether there were any lingering spells, but he did not sense anything.

Raising a hand, Telemain began to mutter rapidly. Mendanbar watched with interest as the magician worked, calling up magical power and shaping it into a loose net that surrounded all three of them.

"There," Telemain said at last. "That should do it." He repossessed the staff from Cimorene and looked at Mendanbar. "Whenever you're ready."

Mendanbar studied the net uncertainly. "Is that all there is to it? Should I aim through one of the holes or through one of the threads?"

"Holes?" Telemain said. "Threads? What are you talking about?"

"This net of yours," Mendanbar said. "The warding spell. Does it matter where I aim?"

"You can *see* the warding spell?" Telemain looked and sounded considerably startled by the very idea.

"It's not *seeing*, exactly," Mendanbar said. "But I can tell where it is and how it's put together."

"Fascinating," Telemain said. "Have you always been able to do that?"

"No. It comes with being King of the Enchanted Forest."

"*Does* it?" Telemain's expression was all eager interest. "Can you do it for any spell? Here, let me try a listening spell, and you see if you can spot it."

"I thought we were supposed to be trying to get to the Enchanted Forest," Cimorene put in pointedly. "Can't you wait and experiment *after* we rescue Kazul?"

"Of course," Telemain said. "Do forgive me. I sometimes get carried away." He nodded apologetically, but Mendanbar thought he sounded disappointed.

"About this net—" Mendanbar reminded him.

"Oh, yes, you wanted to know about aiming." Telemain considered for a moment. "It shouldn't make the least bit of difference."

"Good," said Mendanbar. He drew his sword, and both Telemain and Cimorene jumped. Mendanbar supposed the sword must be leaking again. He pushed careful little dabs of power through the sword to mark Telemain and Cimorene, to be sure that they would come along with him. Then he raised the sword and pointed toward the mountain, where Jack had said the Enchanted Forest lay.

"I think I'll try to take us straight to the palace," he said, and began forming the picture in his mind.

"No, no!" Telemain interrupted. "Do it *exactly* the way you did before. That's the whole point of this exercise."

"I thought the point was to get to the Enchanted Forest," Cimorene muttered.

Mendanbar shrugged. The castle would be a better place from which to try and locate Kazul, since it was at the center—*near* the center—of the Enchanted Forest, but once they were in the forest, getting to the castle would be no trouble. If Telemain wanted to watch an exact duplication of the transportation spell that had dumped them in the ravine, there was no reason not to let him. Releasing his image of the palace, Mendanbar substituted a mental picture of the Green Glass Pool.

He took his time over the image, painstakingly remembering every detail of the rocks and trees and water. When the picture was as clear as he could make it, he took a deep breath and gave the power of the sword a slow, twisting pull.

The mountains and the trees and Jack's queer little house faded to gray ghosts, then melted into mist and were gone. An instant later, the mist vanished. They were standing at the edge of the Green Glass Pool.

"Absolutely fascinating!" Telemain said. "That is, without a doubt, the neatest transportation spell I have ever had the pleasure of utilizing. But I thought you said you had some trouble with it."

"He did, last time," Cimorene said.

"Well, you'd better not put your sword away, then," Telemain said. "I can't tell what the problem was until I see it. You'll just have to do the spell again."

Mendanbar, who had already stuck his sword back in its sheath, shook his head. "I never use the sword to move around the Enchanted Forest. I don't need it."

"By the way, your sword has stopped spraying magic around again," Cimorene said. "I thought you might want to know."

"So it has," Telemain said. "What an intriguing phenomenon."

"That reminds me," Mendanbar said. "The burned-out area I told you about should be right over there. Would you mind taking a look at it, since we're here?"

"Happy to oblige," Telemain replied.

"What about finding Kazul?" Cimorene asked.

"I'll try and locate her while Telemain is examining the clearing," Mendanbar said. "A locating spell takes a while to set up, anyway, so we won't lose any time to speak of, unless looking at the charred spot takes a lot longer than I expect it to."

Cimorene still did not look altogether pleased, but she nodded, and Mendanbar led the way between the enormous trees. There was the burned section, as empty of life and magic as it had been when he had first seen it. Cimorene's expression changed to one of shock and anger, and even Telemain looked shaken.

"I see why you wanted me to look at this," Telemain said.

"So do I," Cimorene agreed.

Setting the wizard's staff under a tree near the edge of the charred area, Telemain walked slowly forward until he reached the spot where the ashes began. Kneeling, he ran his fingers over the dry, dead earth. After a moment, he rose and moved on, into the burned section itself. Little swirls of ash followed him.

For a few minutes, Mendanbar watched the magician work. Then, remembering his promise to Cimorene, he tore his attention away and turned to his own task.

It was a relief to be back in the Enchanted Forest, where magic was nearly automatic. Quickly, Mendanbar sorted through the invisible threads of power, selecting the ones that ran all the way to the farthest edges of the Enchanted Forest. They made quite a bundle, but it was better to do it all at once than to split them up and risk skipping one by accident.

When he was sure he had all the threads he wanted, he looped them around his right wrist and twined his fingers through the strands as they fanned out in all directions. With his left hand, he caught a free-floating filament and wound it into a small ball. He set the ball on the web of unseen tendrils that radiated out from the bundle at his wrist. In his mind, he pictured Kazul and the wizards as he and Cimorene had seen them in Herman's window. Then he gave the invisible ball a flick and sent it rolling rapidly out along the first of the threads.

The ball picked up speed and vanished. Then it was back, bouncing to the next thread and spinning away along the new path. Out and back it went in the blink of an eye, over and over, eliminating one thread each time. And then it went out and did not return.

Mendanbar frowned. That wasn't supposed to happen. If the spell-ball didn't find Kazul, it should come back and hop to the next thread, to check along it. If it *did* find Kazul, it should come back and stop, marking the thread they should follow to lead them to the dragon. Either way, the spell-ball was supposed to come back.

"What is it?" Cimorene said.

Mendanbar looked up, startled, to find Cimorene watching his face closely. "Something's wrong," he told her. "Wait a minute while I try something."

Gently, he wiggled the last thread down which the spell-ball had vanished. He felt a vibration travel the length of the thread, and for a moment he hoped that it was the spell-ball returning. Then, with a high, thin sound like a tight wire breaking, the thread snapped, leaving a long end waving loose in the air in front of him.

"What was *that?*" Telemain said, looking up.

"Something very wrong indeed," Mendanbar said grimly. "You'd better stop that and come over here. We're going to the palace right now."

14

In Which Mendanbar Has
Some Interesting Visitors

Both Cimorene and Telemain stared at Mendanbar for a moment. Then Telemain shrugged. "Very well," he said, dusting ashes from his fingers. "I was nearly finished, in any case, though I can't say that I like all this flitting around."

"Mendanbar, what happened?" Cimorene demanded as Telemain walked out of the burned area and crossed to the tree to get the wizard's staff.

"I'm not sure I can explain," Mendanbar replied. "It has to do with the way I work magic. The spell—Telemain, what is it?"

Telemain had picked up the staff and was gazing down at the ground where it had lain. "I think you'd better come and see for yourself," he said without looking up.

Feeling mildly irritated, Mendanbar went over to join Telemain. His irritation vanished when he saw what the magician was looking at. At the foot of the tree, a strip of moss had turned as brown and dead and brittle as the crumbling remnants within the burned-out area a few feet away. And the strip was the exact size and shape of the wizard's staff.

"Wizards again," Cimorene said in tones of disgust. "It figures."

"It *looks* the same as that part," Mendanbar said cautiously, waving at the dead spot. "But is it?"

"So far as I can determine from a limited visual examination, it is," Telemain said. "If you want absolute certainty, you'll have to give me another couple of hours for tests."

"We don't have a couple of hours," Mendanbar said. "How sure are you, right now, that this wizard's staff has done the same thing to this bit of moss as something did to that whole section over there?"

"And have you any idea how it did it?" Cimorene put in.

"The *how* is very simple," Telemain answered. "The staff is designed to appropriate any unattached magic with which it comes in contact. Magic appears to be a fundamental property of the Enchanted Forest. So when the staff rested for a few minutes in one location, it swallowed up all the magic from that location, leaving it as you see."

"What about that?" Cimorene asked, waving at the

burned area. "What did they do, roll a wizard's staff around on the ground for an hour?"

"Of course not," Telemain said. "It's simply a matter of extending and intensifying the absorption spell. One couldn't maintain such an expansion for very long, but then, one wouldn't have to."

"That's it!" Mendanbar said suddenly.

The other two looked at him blankly. "What's what?" said Cimorene.

"That must be what happened to that locating spell I sent out," Mendanbar explained. "Some wizard's staff sucked it up. That's why it didn't come back."

"Come back?" Telemain said. "You mean your locating spells work on a sort of echo principle? Would you mind demonstrating just how you—"

"Not *now*, Telemain," Cimorene said. She looked at Mendanbar. "Does that mean you know where the wizards are?"

"No, but I think I know how to find out," Mendanbar said. "Ready or not, here we go."

Without waiting for a response, Mendanbar took hold of a thread of magic and pulled. Mist rose and fell, and they were standing in front of the main door to the palace.

"Willin!" Mendanbar shouted, throwing open the door. "Willin, come here. I need—"

He stopped short. Standing in the middle of the entrance hall was a boy of about ten in a blue silk doublet heavily embroidered with gold, a middle-aged man in black velvet with a pinched expression, two cats (one cream-and-silver, the other a long-haired tabby), Morwen, and an extremely harried-looking Willin. The footman who tended the front door was watching them all with the carefully blank face he kept for odd visitors and unusual events. He had had a lot of practice.

"Your Majesty! Oh, thank goodness," said Willin in tones of heartfelt relief. "This woman—these people—"

"Willin."

The elf stopped abruptly and made a visible effort to pull himself together. While he was still working at it, Morwen stepped forward.

"Hello, Cimorene, Mendanbar," she said briskly. "You're back just in time. These people have some very interesting infor—"

"*Morwen?*" Telemain's incredulous voice interrupted from behind Mendanbar. A moment later, the magician pushed his head between Cimorene and Mendanbar to get a better look. "It *is* you. What on earth are you doing in the Enchanted Forest?"

"Living in it," Morwen answered calmly. "As you would know if you bothered to keep up with the doings of your old friends, Telemain."

"I've been busy," Telemain said defensively.

One of the cats made a small growling noise. "Nonsense," Morwen told it. "It's perfectly normal for him to be busy. The question is, has he got anything to show for it?"

Both cats turned their heads and gazed expectantly at Telemain. Mendanbar decided it was time to take a hand in the conversation, before things got so far off track that he'd never get them back on again.

"Telemain has been very helpful," he said. "Morwen, who are these other people?"

"His Royal Highness, Crown Prince Jorillam of Meriambee," Willin said in a loud, formal tone before Morwen could reply. The elf nodded at the boy, who bowed uncertainly.

"And His Royal Highness's uncle and guardian, Prince Rupert," Willin continued. This time, the older man stepped forward to acknowledge the introduction.

"They have come with the witch Morwen"—Willin paused, obviously waiting for Morwen to curtsy. Morwen only looked at him, and after a moment the elf went on—"with the witch Morwen to beg a boon of His Majesty Mendanbar, the King of the Enchanted Forest."

"It's not a big thing, Your Majesty," Prince Rupert said hastily. "Really. If I could just have a minute or two of your time . . ." His voice trailed off in an indistinct murmur.

Mendanbar looked from Prince Rupert to Morwen and back, completely baffled. "I'm in something of a hurry just now," he said at last. "What is it?"

"If we could, ah, discuss the matter in private . . . ," Prince Rupert said with a sidelong look at his nephew.

"Oh, Uncle," said Crown Prince Jorillam in an exasperated tone. He turned to Mendanbar. "He just doesn't want to say straight out that we're lost. And he especially doesn't want to say that the whole reason we came was so he could leave me in the forest and go home and take over my kingdom."

"Jorillam!" Prince Rupert said, plainly horrified.

"Well, it's true, Uncle," the Crown Prince insisted. "And if they're in a hurry, it's better to tell them and not waste time."

"Mrow!" one of the cats agreed emphatically.

"Morwen . . ." Mendanbar said, hoping he did not look or sound as confused as he felt.

The ginger-haired witch shook her head and peered sternly over the top of her glasses at Prince Rupert. "You, sir, are here to tell these people your story with as little shilly-shallying as you can manage. You'd better get started, or I shall be tempted to do something drastic."

"Like what?" asked the Crown Prince, greatly interested. "Could you turn him into a toad?"

"I could," Morwen said repressively, "but I won't. Not yet, anyway. Provided he starts talking."

"Isn't that a bit severe?" Telemain asked, frowning.

"You wouldn't think so if *you'd* been dealing with him for the last two hours," Morwen said.

Cimorene stepped forward and gave Prince Rupert a perfectly charming smile. "Perhaps it would be best if you told us your story," she said.

"Ah, yes, of course," Prince Rupert said, rubbing his hands against each other. "I, um, we, er—"

"It's because of that stupid club Uncle joined," said Crown Prince Jorillam helpfully. "Tell them, Uncle."

"What club is that?" Cimorene asked.

Prince Rupert gave her a hunted look. "The Right Honorable Wicked Stepmothers' Traveling, Drinking, and Debating Society," he said, and sighed. "I've been a member of the Men's Auxiliary for the past fifteen years."

"That would be for Wicked Stepfathers?" Mendanbar guessed, wishing the man would get on with it.

"Yes, though we don't get many of those," Prince

Rupert said. "Mostly, it's Wicked Uncles. You can even join on expectation, if you're not an uncle yet." He sighed again. "That's what I did. I never really expected to be an uncle at all. Rosannon—she's my sister—was under a curse for a hundred years, and I thought I'd be dead when someone finally broke it and married her."

"So you joined this club," Cimorene prompted.

"And it was wonderful!" Prince Rupert's face lit up, remembering. "The places we went to, and the wines, and the discussions! It was everything I dreamed. Only then a smart-alec prince figured out a shortcut and broke the curse, and he and Rosannon got married and had Jorillam here. And *then* the two of them left on some silly quest or other and put me in charge of him."

"It isn't a silly quest!" Jorillam objected. "It's a matter of vital importance to the future of Meriambee."

"You can see my problem," Prince Rupert said earnestly. "If I don't do something really wicked soon, I'll get kicked out of the club. I only have until sunset tomorrow."

"So you brought Crown Prince Jorillam to the Enchanted Forest, intending to abandon him here," Mendanbar said.

"Actually, it was my idea," the Crown Prince put in. "After the other thing didn't work out, we needed to think of something fast."

"Other thing?" said Telemain, fascinated.

Prince Rupert looked embarrassed. "I hired a giant to ravage a village by the eastern border. He was supposed to show up yesterday, and I was all ready to send the documentation in to the club when I got a letter of resignation saying he'd quit that line of work and wouldn't be coming."

Mendanbar and Cimorene exchanged looks.

"Did he say why?" Cimorene asked.

"No, just that he'd done enough pillaging for one giant, thank you all the same, and now he was going to try something new."

"So I said Uncle Rupert should abandon me in the woods," Jorillam said. "That's *much* more wicked than hiring a giant, isn't it? And I'd get to have some adventures, too, instead of sitting home while Mother and Father are off on their quest. Only first we couldn't find the forest, and then we got chased by some wizards, and then we found the forest just in time and lost the wizards, except we got lost, too, and Uncle Rupert wouldn't leave. And then we were captured by a witch and she brought us here. Are you going to throw us in a dungeon?"

"What was that part about *wizards?*" Mendanbar demanded.

"I thought you'd be interested," Morwen said with considerable satisfaction.

"But that was *before* we got to the Enchanted Forest," Prince Rupert said in a bewildered tone. "Why would the King of the Enchanted Forest be interested in that?"

"Never mind," said Mendanbar. "Just tell me what happened."

"Well, we were just coming out of the old Pass of the Dragons," Prince Rupert said. "It cuts straight through the Mountains of Morning to the Enchanted

Forest, and hardly anyone uses it these days, so I thought it would be a good choice. Only things must have changed, because when we came out of the pass we were in a wasteland, and not in the Enchanted Forest at all."

Mendanbar, Telemain, and Cimorene looked at each other. "Describe this wasteland," Mendanbar said.

"It was—it was bare," Rupert told him. "Um, well, bare. No grass or trees or anything. Just . . . just . . ."

"Just bare," Cimorene finished for him. "Did it look burned?"

"Yes, now that you mention it. I didn't examine it closely, you understand, because that was when the wizards came out of the cave and chased us off."

"We had to run for *miles*," Crown Prince Jorillam said with relish. "They almost caught us."

"It was a long way, but it wasn't *miles*," his uncle corrected. "And they lost us as soon as we got to the trees."

The forest must have shifted, thought Mendanbar. *Good for it.* "Thank you very much," he said aloud. "You've been very helpful."

"We have?" Prince Rupert said.

"Does that mean you're not going to throw us in a dungeon?" asked Crown Prince Jorillam, sounding disappointed.

"Not at all," Mendanbar said. "Willin, after we're gone, see that His Royal Highness, here, is made comfortable in one of the dungeons. The one under the North-Northwest Tower, I think." Mendanbar smiled to himself, thinking that it might do the overeager young prince good to climb up and down six flights of stairs to get what he wanted, and it certainly wouldn't do him any harm.

"Of course, Your Majesty," said Willin in tones of perfect understanding. He paused. "May I inquire where you are going and when?"

"To rescue the King of the Dragons," Mendanbar said, "and as soon as possible."

Willin swallowed hard, Prince Rupert choked, and even Morwen looked slightly startled.

"The only question is, what's the best way of doing it," Mendanbar continued. "Any suggestions?"

"We can't just charge in and attack the cave," Cimorene said, frowning. "The wizards could kill Kazul before we got to her. And if the area around the cave looks like that bit you showed us a few minutes ago, it simply won't be possible to sneak up on them."

"What we need is a back way in," Telemain said. "I don't suppose there is one?"

"Every cave in the Enchanted Forest has a back way in," Mendanbar said. "The problem is finding it. Do you know anything about that part of the forest, Morwen?"

"I'm afraid not," Morwen said. She turned to the cats. "Chaos? Jasper? How about you?"

The cats looked at each other, blinked, and looked back at Morwen. "They aren't familiar with the area, either," Morwen said with regret.

Willin coughed. "If I may venture a suggestion, Your Majesty . . ."

"Go ahead," Mendanbar said.

"I believe there is a list of caves, passages, vestibules, and entrances in the Royal Archives," said the elf. "Would you care to examine it?"

"Immediately," Mendanbar replied. "I might have known you'd have a list somewhere with the right information, Willin. I should have asked you at once."

The elf bowed deeply, looking very pleased. "I shall bring it without delay, Your Majesty," he said, and whisked off down the corridor.

"Hey!" cried Crown Prince Jorillam. "Are you going to fight the wizards? Can I come?"

"Yes, we are, and no, you can't," Mendanbar told him. "You're going to be locked in the dungeon, remember?"

"But a fight with wizards is *much* more interesting than being locked in a dungeon," Jorillam complained. "I want to watch."

"Maybe so," Cimorene said. "But that's how it is with dungeons. You aren't supposed to get a choice about whether you're going to be locked up in one, you know."

This was evidently a new idea for the young prince, and he did not look happy about it. "But—"

"But, nothing," Mendanbar said. "I'm the King, and I say you go to the dungeon instead of fighting wizards, and no argument."

"Yes," said Morwen. "We have much more important things to argue about. Such as how to get rid of the wizards once we find them."

"Buckets," said Cimorene. "Lots of buckets, and soap, and lemon juice. Where do you keep your buckets, Mendanbar?"

"Around somewhere," Mendanbar said vaguely.

"I'll have someone bring us a few. Can the three of us carry enough buckets to get rid of all the wizards?"

"Four of us," said Morwen. The cats yowled. "Yes, I know, and of course you're coming, but you can't carry a bucket of soapy water, so for purposes of this discussion it doesn't matter," she told them.

The cats gave her an affronted look, turned their backs, and began making indignant little noises at each other.

"It seems probable that the wizards will be present in force," Telemain said. "They were certainly aware of Prince Rupert's appearance among them this morning, and they may well have detected your unsuccessful locating spell, Mendanbar. Consequently, I would wager that there will be far too many to dispose of by means of your, er, interesting methods, Princess Cimorene."

"We'll bring some buckets along anyway," Mendanbar said. "It can't hurt."

He nodded a summons to the blank-faced footman by the front door. The footman came over at once, and Mendanbar told him to bring half a dozen buckets of soapy water mixed with lemon juice out to the entrance hall immediately. The footman, who had worked at the palace for a long time and was used to peculiar requests, bowed impassively and departed.

"Any other ideas?" Mendanbar asked.

"Can't the witch turn them into toads?" said the Crown Prince.

"I certainly don't object to trying," Morwen said.

Cimorene shook her head. "I don't think it would work. The Society of Wizards has some new spell that soaks up magic. That's what makes the bare spots in the Enchanted Forest."

"I still wish I understood *why* the Society of Wizards is doing all this," Mendanbar said, half to himself. "I suppose it makes sense to try and blame the dragons for burning bits of the Enchanted Forest, but they've been deliberately trying to start a war. That would make almost as much trouble for them as for everyone else."

"Ah, well, but would it?" put in Prince Rupert timidly. "I mean, if these wizards are soaking up magic, they must want it for something."

Cimorene, Morwen, Mendanbar, and Telemain stared at one another in dismay. "Yes, what *are* they using it for?" Cimorene said after a long, thoughtful silence.

"In all probability, to intensify their general enchantments," Telemain said. "Alternatively, to enable themselves to achieve something more substantial than would otherwise be possible."

Prince Rupert looked at the magician blankly. "Oh," he said in a doubtful tone.

"Don't mind him," Morwen said. "He always gets technical when he's talking about spells."

"But what did he *mean?*" the prince asked.

"He meant that the Society of Wizards wants more magic to power their spells," Mendanbar replied. "Or maybe to use in a spell that would be too big for them to work without it."

"Yes, and *that* is an idea I don't care for at all," said Morwen, frowning. "The Society of Wizards is too powerful already, if you ask me."

"You know, if the dragons start fighting with the

Enchanted Forest, any new wasted areas would be blamed on the war," Telemain commented. "The Society of Wizards could absorb considerable quantities of magic before anyone realizes what they are up to."

"That would explain why they're doing this, all right," Mendanbar said. "We have *got* to stop them." Without thinking, he put his hand on the hilt of his sword.

"Mendanbar!" said Cimorene suddenly. "Didn't that wizard say something about you reversing his spell? Not Antorell, the wizard at Jack's house. And you were using the sword. Maybe it can reverse this spell, too."

"It's worth trying," Mendanbar said.

"Not until we have a better idea of exactly what we're up against," Morwen said firmly. "If the King of the Enchanted Forest gets killed trying to rescue the King of the Dragons from the Society of Wizards, goodness only knows *what* will happen."

"We'll sneak in and take a look around," Telemain agreed. "Then we can formulate a plan of action."

"As long as it doesn't take too long," Cimorene muttered. "This isn't some kind of experiment, where we can take our time and try again. If those wizards figure out that someone is trying to rescue Kazul . . ."

Mendanbar tried to smile reassuringly at her. "I don't see how they—ah, Willin! Did you find that list? Good! Then let's all go into the parlor and look at it. The sooner we're done, the sooner we can be on our way."

15

In Which Everyone Argues

❦

Willin's list was remarkably clear and well organized. Once they found the section headed "Caves and Caverns Near the Mountains of Morning," it was only a matter of a few minutes before they discovered the listing for the Cave of Stone Icicles, the only cave at the western end of the Pass of the Dragons. As Mendanbar had predicted, there was a back way into it. A tunnel started from the bottom of the Crystal Falls and wound around under the hills and forest until it reached a crack at the rear of the cave.

"This doesn't look as if it will be hard at all," Cimorene said. "Let's go."

"Right," said Mendanbar. "This shouldn't take

long. I'll be back in an hour or so. Willin, take care of everyone while I'm gone—you know, refreshments and things."

"Wait a minute!" Cimorene said, her voice rising above startled objections from everyone else. "You're not going without me."

"But—"

"I am Kazul's Chief Cook and Librarian," Cimorene said firmly. "It's my job to help rescue her."

"I suppose so," Mendanbar said, "but all I'm going to do is sneak in and look at the wizards, and then sneak out again."

"That's all you *think* you're going to do, but what if something goes wrong?"

"Exactly," Morwen said. "You should have someone with you. Several someones, in fact."

"I'm real good at sneaking," Crown Prince Jorillam put in eagerly. "And I want to see a dragon up close."

"No, you don't," Mendanbar said. "Morwen, are you trying to tell me you want to come along as well?"

"No," Morwen said, looking at him sternly over the tops of her glasses. "I'm telling you I'm going to come whether you like it or not. Kazul is my friend, and besides, I want a crack at those wretched wizards."

"We aren't going to do anything to the wizards until we know more about what we're up against," Mendanbar said, feeling harried.

"Then how come you wanted those buckets of soapy water?" Crown Prince Jorillam demanded.

"Just in case," Mendanbar said. "This is only to find out what the wizards are doing and how many of them there are."

"Which is precisely why I must accompany you," Telemain put in.

"Not you, too!"

Telemain frowned at him. "You don't seem to realize what a priceless opportunity this is," the magician said. "It is entirely possible that we shall be able to observe the Society of Wizards in the very act of casting their magic-absorbing spells. Since they are extremely secretive about their methods, this may be the only chance we have of studying their techniques."

"It isn't worth the risk," Mendanbar said.

"Not to you, perhaps," Telemain told him. "I, however, intend to take full advantage of these circumstances. One way or another, I am going to get a look at those wizards." He leaned the wizard's staff against the wall and folded his arms stubbornly.

"Yeah, and then we melt 'em!" Crown Prince Jorillam said enthusiastically.

"You are *not* coming with us," Mendanbar told him.

"But I'm real, real good at sneaking," Jorillam said. "Tell them, Uncle!"

"He is," Prince Rupert said earnestly. "And I'll keep an eye on him so he won't get in your way."

Mendanbar stared at him. "No, you won't. Because you aren't coming with me, either. I am going to sneak into the Cave of Stone Icicles *by myself*."

"No, you're not," said everyone at once. Morwen's two cats glanced up, then went back to washing their tails. Mendanbar got the distinct impression that the only reason they hadn't joined in the general outcry was that they thought it was beneath them to argue.

"It is inappropriate for the King of the Enchanted Forest to embark on a mission to the King of the Dragons without a formal escort," Willin added.

"You want me to take all these people along as a formal escort?" Mendanbar said incredulously. "Really, Willin—"

"Not at all," the elf replied. "They are all persons of distinction, and it would not be suitable for any of them to take a position as a formal escort to Your Majesty. Properly, only those of your subjects already in Your Majesty's employ may make up such a retinue. Due to Your Majesty's general dislike of formality, we have very few such persons available at present."

"What are you suggesting?" Mendanbar asked with a sinking feeling.

"That I am the only possible person who can accompany Your Majesty in this capacity," Willin said.

"If he gets to go, so do I!" Crown Prince Jorillam cried.

"Not without me," Prince Rupert said, setting his jaw. "I don't know anything about this business with the dragons and wizards, but Jorillam is my responsibility. Until I lose him in the forest, that is."

"And Kazul is *my* responsibility," Cimorene said.

"Like it or not, I am going to get a look at those spells," Telemain stated flatly.

"Those wizards have caused me a lot of trouble, what with one thing and another," Morwen pointed out. "I intend to cause them a bit of trouble back."

"It is necessary to Your Majesty's dignity that Your Majesty take a proper escort with you," Willin put in.

"QUIET!" Mendanbar said.

Everyone stopped talking. Willin looked utterly astonished. Jorillam had a wary expression, and Prince Rupert and Telemain both looked mildly taken aback. Morwen's eyes gleamed approvingly behind her glasses. Cimorene looked momentarily startled, but then she smiled.

Mendanbar took a deep breath. First things first. "Crown Prince Jorillam."

"Yes?"

"You are not coming on this expedition. You will stay here, at my castle, until I return. In the dungeon, just as you requested."

"But it's not fair," Jorillam said. "I didn't know *then* that you were going to go fight wizards. And that elf—"

"Willin is one of my people, and a native of the Enchanted Forest," Mendanbar said. "You aren't. Don't bother arguing; you don't get a choice. I'm the King here, remember."

Jorillam gave him a sulky nod.

"Prince Rupert," Mendanbar went on, "you were quite right to say that your nephew needs watching. You will stay here and keep an eye on him while I'm gone."

"Certainly, Your Majesty," Prince Rupert said with a relieved sigh. "If you say so."

"I'm afraid I can't bring you with me, either, Willin," Mendanbar said, turning to his steward. "Somebody has to take care of our visitors, you know, and you're the only possible person."

Willin hesitated, plainly torn. "It is my duty to serve Your Majesty regardless of the danger."

"I appreciate your willingness to accompany me," Mendanbar assured him. "I feel, however, that you would serve me better here. Now, please take these two guests to the North-Northwest Tower dungeon and see that they get some refreshments."

"As Your Majesty commands," Willin said, bowing. He gestured to Prince Rupert and Crown Prince Jorillam, and led them away.

Well, that takes care of them, *anyway*, Mendanbar thought as the three rounded a bend in the corridor and vanished from sight. The rest wouldn't be that easy. He looked over and saw Morwen, Cimorene, and Telemain standing side by side, wearing identical expressions of stubbornness, and he sighed. He supposed he could accidentally-on-purpose forget to include them in the transportation spell, but somehow he didn't think that would stop them. Not when one was a witch, one a magician, and one an experienced dragon's princess.

"Don't even bother trying to talk us out of it," Cimorene warned. "You'll only waste more time."

"You're probably right," Mendanbar said at last. "And anyway, I suspect I really *should* have some help with me, just in case."

"Very sensible of you," Morwen told him.

"Yes, well, let's get our buckets and go," Mendanbar said uncomfortably.

The four of them collected buckets of soapy water from the imperturbable castle footman. Cimorene and Telemain took two each, but Mendanbar only took one, because he wanted to keep one hand free in case he needed his sword. Morwen also took only one bucket.

She did not explain, and her expression dared anyone to comment. No one did.

The footman left, removing Telemain's staff along the way. "Be sure you put that somewhere safe," Telemain called after him.

Mendanbar looked around one last time, checking to make sure everyone was finally ready, then twitched the strands of power and transported them all to the foot of the Crystal Falls.

They appeared on the slippery bank of a narrow stream. A little farther on, the Crystal Falls poured in a shining curtain down the side of a sheer cliff of black glass. The water foamed and swirled at the foot of the falls, forming a small, restless pool, then rushed down the channel at their feet and dashed on into the deeper parts of the Enchanted Forest. The noise of the falling water was tremendous, and the air had a clean, sharp smell.

Mendanbar looked around to see that everyone was there and that no one had spilled the soapy water. He noticed, without surprise, that the two cats had come along, even though he had not specifically included them in the transportation spell. Cats were like that.

"Which way is the tunnel entrance?" Cimorene asked. She had to shout to make herself heard over the roar of the waterfall.

"Over there," Mendanbar shouted back, waving at a clump of fir trees near the foot of the cliff. "Watch your step."

"What did you say?" Telemain yelled.

"He said, 'Watch your step,' " Cimorene replied at the top of her lungs.

Telemain nodded, and they moved cautiously away from the water-slick bank of the stream. The cats had already moved out of range of the mist billowing up from the base of the waterfall. When the rest of the group caught up to them, the two cats gave Mendanbar looks of deep reproach, as if to imply that he should have more sense than to set everyone down so close to such a damply uncomfortable spot.

The tunnel entrance was a narrow crack in the side of the cliff, hidden behind the clump of firs. The cats trotted through it and vanished into the darkness. Morwen gazed after them with a thoughtful expression on her face.

"I don't suppose anyone remembered to bring a light?" Cimorene said, eying the crack with evident misgiving.

Telemain smiled and said three words that crackled in the air. A small globe of golden light appeared above his head. "I'll go first, so the rest of you can see where you're stepping," he said, smiling with a trace of smugness.

"And what do you think will happen when we get near the wizards and their magic-absorbing spell gets hold of your little glow-ball?" Morwen said sharply. "You're not thinking, Telemain."

"I suppose you have a better idea?"

Morwen pushed her glasses firmly into place, set down her bucket of soapy water, and reached into one of her long, loose sleeves. She pulled out a small lantern and set it on the ground. Then she reached into the other sleeve, from which she pulled a flint striker and a long splinter of wood. Expertly, she struck a spark and lit the splinter, then used the splinter to light the lantern. She blew the splinter out, stuffed it and the flint back into her sleeve, and smiled at the surprise on everyone else's face.

"I thought we might be needing this," she said. Picking up the lantern and the bucket, she started for the mouth of the tunnel.

"Hang on a minute," Mendanbar said. "I should go first. Would you give me the lantern, Morwen?"

"Only if you don't dawdle," Morwen responded. "My cats are in there."

"Of course. You come next, then, and Telemain after you. Cimorene can come last. That way we'll have a light between every two people."

Cimorene did not look happy about these arrangements, but Mendanbar did not give anyone time to argue. As soon as Morwen nodded, he took the lantern and started into the crack. It was only wide enough for one of them at a time to edge sideways, and the ground was covered with shattered rock, which made the footing treacherous. Juggling the lantern and his bucket back and forth from hand to hand, Mendanbar tried to see what lay ahead of him while still giving Morwen enough light to follow. Progress was slow, and he began to wonder whether the whole tunnel was going to be as narrow and difficult as this beginning.

"Maybe we would have been better off charging at the main entrance," he muttered to himself.

After what seemed a very long time, but was probably only a few minutes, the tunnel widened. The piles of shattered rock became fewer, then ceased altogether. Mendanbar heaved a sigh of relief and stopped to let the others catch up.

Morwen was the first. "Good," she said as she clambered over the last of the rock piles, balancing carefully to avoid spilling her bucket. "I was beginning to think that rocky stuff was never going to end. Any sign of my cats?"

"It would be more reasonable to ask whether there is any sign of the wizards," Telemain said, following Morwen into the wider part of the tunnel. There was a large wet spot down one side of his many-pocketed vest; apparently he had not been as careful with his buckets as Morwen.

"I haven't seen a trace of the wizards," Mendanbar said, "but the cats have been by here." He pointed at two small trails of footprints leading down the tunnel.

"Thank goodness that's over," Cimorene said as she emerged from the narrow section of the tunnel to join them. "Why are you all just standing here? The Cave of Stone Icicles is a lot farther on."

As this was undeniably true, they set off again. There was still not room for all four of them to stand in a line, but at least now they could walk two by two without difficulty. Somehow, Cimorene ended up walking with Mendanbar in the front. Mendanbar was not sure whether to be glad or sorry. He enjoyed walking with Cimorene, even if they did not dare to talk much; the wizards might have someone listening for odd noises. On the other hand, being in front meant that he and Cimorene were the ones the wizards would attack first. Mendanbar did not like the idea of anyone attacking Cimorene, although he knew she could take care of herself.

He had some time to consider this, for the tunnel was long and winding, but he found it hard to concentrate with Cimorene walking so close beside him. He discovered that he wanted to put his arm around her as they walked—the one carrying the bucket of water, not the lantern—but somehow that didn't seem like the right thing to do when they were supposed to be watching out for wizards. He had never met a princess like Cimorene before. He had never met *anyone* like Cimorene before. She was smart and brave and kind and loyal, and he liked her. In fact, he liked her a great deal. In fact—

Suddenly, the light around Mendanbar dimmed. He stopped and glanced over his shoulder. The little globe that had been hovering over Telemain's head had gone out.

"Telemain?" Mendanbar whispered.

"I didn't turn it off," Telemain whispered back. "We must be getting near the wizards."

Mendanbar nodded without surprise—the atmosphere in the tunnel felt dry and magicless, and though they were still within the Enchanted Forest, he could no longer sense threads of power floating invisibly in the air. He swallowed, hoping he would not have to do any spells in a hurry.

"Keep close," he whispered to Telemain and Morwen, and slowly started forward once more.

The tunnel bent sharply to the left, then right, and without further warning opened out into a forest of stone pillars. A glimmer of light showed between the stones, and they could hear a mumble of voices in the distance.

Hastily, Mendanbar covered the lantern with a corner of his cloak, so that it only lit the area just in front of his feet. Cimorene dropped back. After a moment, she put her hand on his shoulder, and Mendanbar wondered briefly what she had done with the bucket. She gave his shoulder a brief squeeze to indicate that Morwen and Telemain had taken their places. Then he heard her pick the bucket up again.

Carefully, Mendanbar edged through the pillars toward the light and voices.

As they drew nearer, Mendanbar began to understand what the voices were saying.

"I don't like this," grumbled one. "We've wasted too much time already. We should just take her outside, dose her with dragonsbane, and leave her for someone to find."

"Stop complaining, Dizenel," replied a smooth voice, and Mendanbar frowned as he recognized Zemenar's fluid tones. "I have told you a hundred times how foolish that would be," Zemenar went on. "I am not going to tell you for the hundred and first."

"He's right, though," another voice said. "Someone is going to notice us pretty soon, and then where will all our planning be?"

"Someone already has," a fourth voice rasped. "What about those two this morning?"

"A couple of adventurers," Zemenar said dismissively. "They don't matter."

"They got away, didn't they? If they tell someone what they saw—"

"They won't," Zemenar said.

"How can you be sure of that?"

Zemenar gave a snort. "Because of who they are. Can't you recognize a Wicked Uncle when you see one? He was probably here to drop the boy somewhere in the Enchanted Forest. *He* isn't going to tell anyone about us. And even if he does, what of it? Everyone knows odd things happen in the Enchanted Forest. His story will only be one more."

Mendanbar was at the end of the stone columns, close enough to see the wizards if he peeked around a pillar. There were ten of them, grouped about a small table at one side of an enormous cavern. Zemenar and two others were seated; the rest leaned against the wall of the cave or stood in clumps close by. High above the wizards, hundreds of long, cone-shaped columns hung like stone icicles from the ceiling. Four torches dangled from iron brackets on the wall and a lamp stood in the center of the table, throwing shadows like dark fangs from the hanging rocks.

Partway across the cavern, a pale golden glow cut across the shadows like a drawn curtain. On the other side of the glow was a dragon, her wings folded along her back, her eyes narrowed to slits. Mendanbar recognized her at once, even without Cimorene's hiss. She was the same dragon they had seen in the magic window at the dwarf's house—Kazul, the King of the Dragons.

16

In Which Mendanbar Cleans Up

Mendanbar blew out the lantern and set it on the floor. They didn't need it anymore anyway. They were near enough to see by the light of the wizards' torches, even in the shadows. Carrying their buckets, Cimorene, Morwen, and Telemain slipped behind nearby pillars as another wizard came around the corner from the far end of the cave.

"Most gracious and powerful Head Wizard," he said, bowing to Zemenar. "We've checked everything at least twice. There's no one outside and no sign of anyone coming. That spell Xinamon felt before must have been some sort of normal variation."

Behind the pillars, Mendanbar winced. The wizards *had* noticed the locating spell he had sent out earlier. Cimorene frowned and shook her head at him, but he wasn't sure what she meant by that. Morwen scowled at them both and put her finger to her lips.

"Possibly," Zemenar replied. "I don't want to take any chance, though. The King of the Enchanted Forest has a certain amount of magic, and we don't fully understand it. Call in a few more wizards, just to make sure."

"If you don't want to take chances, we ought to use up the dragon now and get out of here," Dizenel said.

"I'm with you," the most recent arrival agreed. "Dragons make me nervous. Are you sure she can't get out?"

"If she could, she'd have done so right away," Zemenar said. "Don't worry about it. We've put the power of at least an acre of the Enchanted Forest into building that shield, and no one can lower it except us."

"Are you sure?" the wizard persisted.

"Take a closer look, if you're not satisfied," Zemenar said, waving at the glow.

"It *is* impressive," the wizard said, moving nearer. "But with a spell this new, how can you be positive— Say, what's that?"

At their companion's change in tone, the wizards' heads swiveled to look at Kazul. For a frozen moment, no one spoke. Then a wizard at the back said, "It's a cat."

Mendanbar glanced sideways in time to see Morwen shake her head and take a firmer grip on her bucket of soapy water. He grimaced. They had only six buckets of soapy water among them, and there were already eleven wizards in the cave. If it came to a fight, they would be badly outnumbered.

"How did a cat get inside the shield?" another wizard asked. "It wasn't there yesterday."

"It wasn't there a few hours ago," Dizenel said. "Where did it come from?"

"Spread out and search the cave," Zemenar commanded, rising. "And bring in the dragonsbane. Someone's snooping."

The wizards fanned out across the cavern and started toward the forest of pillars. There was no way Mendanbar and the others could get away without being seen, even if they had been willing to abandon Kazul to her fate. Mendanbar drew his sword. Soapy water or not, he felt better with a weapon in his hand.

As the first wizard reached the pillars, he jerked in surprise, then raised his staff. Before he could release whatever spell he had planned, a shower of soapy water drenched him from head to foot. The wizard shrieked loudly.

"Blast you six ways from next Wednesday!" he shouted as he began to melt. "This is the second time you've liquefied me! May you and your pet dragon and your triple-cursed wash water turn purple with orange spots and fall down a bottomless pit!"

The other wizards stopped in their tracks. "It's Cimorene!" one of them said nervously.

"That's *Princess* Cimorene, to you," Cimorene said, stepping out from behind a pillar. She held her second bucket in plain sight, ready to throw.

"Stay back," Zemenar ordered. "Blast her from a distance."

"Cowards!" Cimorene taunted, and ducked behind another of the stone columns. "Come and get me!"

It wasn't going to work, Mendanbar told himself, taking a firmer grip on his sword. Zemenar was too clever to let his wizards chase Cimorene into the maze of stone. They would stay at a safe distance and throw bolts of power into the pillars until they destroyed the maze or killed everyone in it, or both.

Three more wizards came running in. Zemenar stopped them with a gesture. The rest of the wizards backed away from the pillars and lined up across the width of the cave.

"Now, then," the Head Wizard said, lifting his staff and pointing it at the pillar Cimorene had ducked behind. "Like this."

Mendanbar felt magic swell around the end of the staff. An instant later, before he had time to reach for the magic himself, the spell shot forward and exploded, shattering the pillar and sending chips of rock flying in all directions.

"Ow!" Cimorene's voice cried from somewhere in the shadows.

Without thinking, Mendanbar stepped out from behind his pillar, bucket in one hand, sword in the other, into full view of the wizards. "Over here!" he called. If he could distract them for a minute or two, perhaps Cimorene could get safely behind another column.

"Mendanbar!" For an instant, Zemenar looked

thoroughly startled. Then he smiled nastily. "How nice to see you. I've been hoping you would turn up, so we could finish this little business at last."

As he spoke, Zemenar stepped forward and shifted his staff to point at Mendanbar. Mendanbar raised his sword and stayed where he was. He felt magic building around the staff once more and decided not to wait to find out what Zemenar intended it to become. Instead, he reached out through the sword and touched the wizard's spell, the same way he touched the magic threads of the Enchanted Forest.

It was much easier to do here than it had been in the Mountains of Morning. The sword sopped up the spell in an instant. Mendanbar could sense the channels of power Zemenar had been using to feed his spell, and he touched those, too, and pulled. The sword obligingly drank them in.

"What are you doing?" Zemenar cried in astonishment, lowering his staff. His hair stood out around his head, as wild and tangled as the magical mess he'd left on the floor of Mendanbar's castle.

"I'm stopping you," Mendanbar said. His whole arm tingled with the power the sword had absorbed. If he could just think of the right thing to do with it . . .

"And a good thing, too," Morwen said from several pillars over. "You're too greedy for your own good, or anyone else's, for that matter."

"I am not greedy," Zemenar protested angrily. "I have every right to—"

"You're greedy, all right," Cimorene said from just

behind Mendanbar. "And you wouldn't know what to do with all the power you want even if you got it. Just look at you! Your hair's like a bird's nest."

Zemenar scowled. Mendanbar stared at him without really seeing him, trying to remember why Cimorene's words sounded familiar.

"The gargoyle!" he said suddenly. "Why didn't I think of that before?"

"What gargoyle?" one of the wizards asked.

"Never mind him," Zemenar said. "He's only trying to distract us. All together, now: blast them!"

The line of wizards raised their staffs. Mendanbar grinned and twisted the mass of power in the sword, just as he had done two days earlier when he had grown tired of the gargoyle's complaints. Soapy water spurted out of the empty air in front of the wizards in a hard, fast stream, as if it were being pumped through an invisible hose. The foaming spray washed over the entire line, thoroughly soaking them all. Puddles grew rapidly on the stones underfoot, and wizards shouted and slid on the suddenly slippery floor. Several of them dropped their staffs to rub at their eyes, which had apparently gotten soap in them. None of them melted.

Mendanbar felt a moment of panic. He'd been sure that his magically created soapy water would work just as well as the buckets they had hauled with them from the castle, but it didn't seem to be doing anything. The wizards would get themselves together any minute, and what would he do then?

"Did you remember the lemon juice?" Cimorene said in his ear.

"Oh, right," said Mendanbar. He twisted the

power again, and another spray of soapy water (this time smelling strongly of lemon) squirted over the wizards. To Mendanbar's considerable relief, they collapsed into gooey puddles, one after another. In another moment, there were no wizards left in the cave at all, only staffs, soggy robes, and a great deal of water and soapsuds.

Mendanbar studied the puddles, then set his bucket of soapy water on the ground. It didn't look as if he'd be needing it anymore. He kept his sword out, however, since he didn't know how many more wizards might still be outside.

"Fascinating," said Telemain. He moved forward and knelt at the edge of a puddle. "This mess appears to be mainly the liquefying agent."

"It does?" Cimorene asked.

"He means it's mostly soapy water," Mendanbar said.

"And a good thing, too, or it would take forever to clean up," Morwen said. "Wizards are a nuisance even when they're gone."

"It's a pity it isn't permanent," Cimorene said. "I'd like to get rid of that Zemenar once and for all."

"Removing their staffs will delay their reappearance," Telemain said. "I suggest we do so before we leave."

"Good idea," Morwen said. She picked her way between puddles and began collecting the wizards' staffs. Telemain went back to studying the puddle.

Cimorene turned to Mendanbar. "Now, if Kazul can just—oh, no!"

Mendanbar followed Cimorene's gaze. The glowing, golden shield spell still blocked half of the cavern, imprisoning Kazul.

There was a long silence. Then Cimorene said, "Telemain, were those wizards right when they said they were the only ones who could take down that spell?"

"What's that?" Telemain said, looking up. "Really, *must* you interrupt so constantly? I'm never going to get anything finished at this rate."

"But think of all the interesting things you're finding out," Mendanbar said. "This shield, for instance. Have you ever seen anything like it before?"

"Now that you mention it, no," Telemain replied, scrambling to his feet. "Let me look at it."

"That was the idea," Cimorene muttered.

They all watched while Telemain examined the shield. He walked from one end to the other, then put a hand gingerly against the glow and pushed. When nothing seemed to happen, he twisted one of his rings twice and touched it to the glow.

"Can you get rid of it?" Cimorene asked.

"I don't know yet," Telemain said. "I'm still checking the parameters of the primary enchantment."

"Oh."

The magician twisted a different ring and touched it to the glow. This time there was a spark. "Ah!" Telemain said in a satisfied tone. "I suspected as much."

"Well, are you going to tell us about it?" Morwen said as she dropped a load of wizards' staffs in a pile against the wall.

"It's a self-sustaining barrier produced by a recirculation of the initial power input," Telemain explained. "Because of the rotation effect, most physical substances cannot pass through the shield in either direction. Unlike the majority of spells, this one needs no exterior energy source, so the usual procedures for dismantling such sorceries would be completely ineffective."

"What does that mean?" Cimorene demanded.

"The spell keeps itself up, we can't get in or out, and we don't have any way of getting rid of it," Mendanbar translated.

"Then how did the cat get in?" Cimorene asked, pointing at Morwen's large silver-and-cream cat, which had climbed onto Kazul's back and lay curled up between her wings.

"Cats are like that," Morwen said. "When he comes out, I'll ask him how he did it, if you want me to, but don't expect too much in the way of an answer. Cats enjoy being mysterious."

"I don't care what they enjoy," Cimorene said. "We have to get Kazul out of there, and if that cat can help—"

"It is unlikely," Telemain interrupted, stepping back from the glow. "The cat's method of moving through the barrier is, in all probability, useless to anyone else. Fortunately, we have other resources."

"We do?"

Telemain looked at Mendanbar. "While I have not had a chance to make a thorough and complete examination of that extremely intriguing weapon you carry, I have observed enough to determine that its function is fundamentally antithetical to wizards and their magic. A straightforward penetration appears quite possible and would disrupt the recirculation effect, resulting in the collapse of the self-sustaining mechanism."

"What?" said Cimorene.

"Really, Telemain, must you?" said Morwen.

"Right," said Mendanbar. He took three steps forward and stuck his sword into the glowing spell.

A jolt of power ran up his arm and the globe of light flashed brighter than the sun. Mendanbar's eyes were dazzled by the flare, so he couldn't see anything except purple spots, but he heard a loud roar, the angry hiss of a cat, and the sound of scales on stone, so he was sure the barrier was gone.

"Kazul," Cimorene called from behind him. "It's all right. It's not wizards, it's us."

"And about time," a deep, unfamiliar voice said. "Hello, Cimorene, Morwen. It's nice to see you again. Who are these others?"

"This is Mendanbar, the King of the Enchanted Forest," Cimorene answered, and Mendanbar felt her hand on his shoulder. "He's the one who let you out. Over there is Telemain. He's a magician, and he figured out how to do it."

"Greetings, Your Majesty," Mendanbar said, blinking. The purple spots began to fade at last, and he found himself staring into the green-gold eyes of an enormous female dragon. He only just managed to keep himself from backing up automatically. "Pleased to meet you."

"Under the circumstances, most definitely so am I," said the dragon with a smile that showed a large number of sharp-looking silver teeth. "How did you manage it?"

"Weren't you watching?" Cimorene asked.

"Watching what?" Kazul replied. "I couldn't see a thing except what was inside that blasted bubble with me."

"We could see you."

"The shielding spell was unidirectional," Telemain put in. "The external absorptive effect would enhance its efficiency."

Kazul gave Telemain a hard look and smiled again, this time showing *all* of her teeth. "What was that again?"

Telemain looked at Kazul. Then he looked at Mendanbar. He frowned in concentration, and finally he said carefully, "The shield was a one-way spell. It soaked up everything that tried to get in from outside and used the energy to make itself stronger."

"Very good," Morwen said. "I was beginning to think you were hopeless."

"I haven't the slightest idea what you're talking about," Telemain said with dignity.

A yowl of complaint made them all turn their heads. The cream-and-silver cat was standing at the edge of the wet, soapy, lemon-scented area where the wizards had melted, shaking his front paws one at a time and eying the water with extreme disfavor.

"Too bad," Morwen told the cat. "If you hadn't sneaked in and attracted their attention, Mendanbar might not have had to be quite so extravagant with the spray. You'll have to get across it by yourself. Where's Chaos?"

The cat blinked disdainfully and began washing his right paw. Kazul snorted softly. "If you want a ride, climb up," she told the cat. "But you'd better hurry, because I'm leaving now."

Kazul rose to her feet, shaking her wings. The cat looked up from his washing, then took two bounds and leaped from the top of a projecting rock. He disappeared behind Kazul's shoulder, and there was a brief sound of claws scraping against scales. Then the cat appeared on Kazul's back, riding comfortably between the dragon's wings and looking tremendously pleased with himself.

"Wait a minute," Mendanbar said as the dragon started toward the other end of the cave. "There may be more wizards out there."

"Good," said Kazul without slowing down at all. "Four days is a long time to spend inside a blank bubble, and I owe them one. Besides, I'm *hungry*."

"I should think so!" Cimorene said, following the dragon. "Didn't they give you anything to eat?"

"No, and I wouldn't have taken it if they had," Kazul said. Her voice became muffled as her head turned the corner at the far end of the cave. "For all I knew, those mumble mumble could have mumble dragonsbane in everything. I mumble mumble end up like Tokoz."

"But if there are more wizards—," Mendanbar began, then gave up and hurried after Cimorene. Clearly, neither she nor Kazul was going to listen to him, and if there *were* more wizards outside it would be better if he—and his sword—were there to help.

17

*In Which Mendanbar Grows Some Trees
and Makes a Wicked Suggestion*

*T*here were, however, no wizards outside the cave.
There was only an enormous stretch of barren land that
looked as if it had been burned. Morwen's long-haired
tabby cat sat in the ashes several feet from the mouth
of the cave, surveying the waste with evident
disapproval.

"There you are," Morwen said to the cat as she
joined Cimorene and Mendanbar by Kazul's left shoulder. "Any sign of more wizards?"

The cat meowed.

"Good," said Morwen. "Did any of the others get
away?"

The cat made a growling noise.

"Very good," said Morwen. She turned to Mendanbar. "Can you keep them from interrupting us by accident?"

"I don't think so," Mendanbar said. "There isn't any magic here for me to work with." He was horrified at the extent of the destruction. How was he going to fix it?

"So *this* is how they did it," Telemain's voice said from behind Mendanbar. He sounded pleased, as if he had just solved a very difficult puzzle. "I'd been wondering."

"Did what?" Mendanbar asked.

"Established that shield spell," Telemain said. "The power involved was clearly several factors beyond the generating capacity of—"

Kazul turned her head and looked at Telemain.

Telemain coughed. "There weren't enough wizards to have done it by themselves."

"Power," Mendanbar said, half to himself. "They sucked all the magic out of this whole area and put it in the shield. Where did it go when the shield disappeared?"

"Into your sword, of course," said Telemain, as if that were so obvious that everyone should have realized it without his saying anything.

"And the sword is linked to the forest," Mendanbar said. "And this is part of the forest, or should be. So . . ."

"So all you have to do is use the sword to put the magic back where it belongs," Cimorene finished.

"Theoretically, that should work fine," Telemain said, frowning. "But the practical applications aren't always that easy."

"Nonsense," said Cimorene. "That sword turned a whole patch of the Mountains of Morning into a bit of the Enchanted Forest when we were having all that trouble getting here. Mendanbar pulled it back into the sword then; all he has to do now is turn that spell around and push magic out. Try it, Mendanbar."

Slowly, Mendanbar lowered the tip of the sword until it touched the ashes. He couldn't feel anything at first. Then he realized that he was trying to reach outside himself for the threads of magic that always floated around him in the Enchanted Forest. And in this wasteland there were no threads. He frowned. Closing his eyes, he concentrated on the sword instead.

That felt more promising. He could sense power crackling along the length of the blade, lots of power, but he did not think it would be enough. He stretched deeper, using his experience outside the Enchanted Forest to pull together every last bit of magic he could reach. It was still not enough.

"I don't think I can do it, Cimorene," he muttered.

"You can, too," Cimorene said, and put her hand on his shoulder encouragingly. "Try again."

As she touched his shoulder, Mendanbar felt it come—not just magic, not only power, but all the magic and power of the Enchanted Forest itself. It washed over him, and as it did he saw patterns in it, patterns that were the threads he manipulated to work magic in the forest. And he saw how to shift the pattern just a little, filling it in with the power stolen from the forest and stored in the sword, to repair the damage the wizards had done. Without thinking, he did it.

He heard an astonished gasp from Cimorene, a

snort from Kazul, a low whistle from Telemain, and a surprised noise from one of the cats.

"Well!" said Morwen.

Mendanbar opened his eyes. A thick carpet of moss, greener than Kazul's scales, spread out in all directions from the cave mouth. Massive oaks and beeches with copper leaves stood so close together that it was hard to see more than a little way into the shadows below them, packing every part of what had been a burned-out waste moments before. All around, Mendanbar could feel threads of magic hovering in the air, ready to use for more ordinary spells.

No one said anything for a long moment. Then Telemain tore his gaze away from the restored forest and turned to Mendanbar.

"Could you do that again, slowly, so I can analyze it?" he asked.

Despite Telemain's urging, Mendanbar refused to repeat the spell immediately, though he did offer to let the magician watch when he went to clean up the barren area near the Green Glass Pool. Then Telemain wanted to stay and investigate the melted wizards some more, but Morwen and Cimorene insisted that this was a bad idea, and eventually he gave in. He was inclined to be sulky about it until Morwen pointed out that he had fourteen more wizards' staffs to study, including one that had belonged to the Head Wizard. It cheered him up enormously.

"You're quite right," he told Morwen. "Those wizards will get themselves back together before long, and once they do, they'll come looking for their staffs. If I don't examine the staffs before then, I'll lose my chance. I can always melt another wizard later and study the disintegration process then." He hurried back into the cave, reappearing a moment later with his arms full of wizards' staffs.

"Be careful with those!" Mendanbar said as Telemain came out onto the moss-covered ground.

"They are unlikely to be a source of difficulty without intelligent guidance," Telemain said reprovingly. "So long as the wizards are not in contact with them, they are merely passive instruments of assimilation. There's nothing to worry about."

"Yes, there is," Cimorene put in. "If you drop them, Mendanbar will have a lot of ugly brown marks on his nice new moss. And if they can do that, there's no telling what else they might do."

"Wizards store spells in their staffs," Morwen said, nodding. "You can't always be sure what will set one off."

Telemain looked at them with annoyance. "I suppose you'd rather I left them here. Have you no spirit of scientific investigation?"

"Not where wizards are concerned," Cimorene muttered.

"Nonsense," Morwen said. "I'm just as curious as you are, Telemain, but I never heard that a spirit of scientific inquiry precluded taking intelligent precautions."

"Oh, I see," said Telemain. "Why didn't you just say so in the first place?"

While the others talked, Mendanbar studied the staffs, keeping a careful watch on the threads of Enchanted Forest magic that were nearest to Telemain. To his surprise, the threads showed no tendency to drift toward the magician or wind themselves into knots around the staffs he carried. Apparently, Telemain was right—the staffs would only be a minor nuisance as long as their wizards weren't carrying them. He resolved to mention this to Telemain later. Perhaps Telemain could even help him find a way to deal with the problems the staffs caused when they *did* have their wizards with them.

A few minutes later, when Kazul was satisfied that there were no wizards left in the area, Mendanbar took them all back to the castle with a quick spell. He was relieved that the wizards' staffs caused no trouble, and pleased to discover that transporting a dragon was no harder than transporting anyone else.

They materialized in the castle courtyard, just inside the moat. Willin, who had apparently been watching for their arrival, came hurrying out to meet them.

"Welcome home, Your Majesty," the elf said with evident relief. Mendanbar noticed that he'd dug up a formal uniform somewhere, all sky-blue velvet and dusty gold braid. "May I assume that your mission was a success?"

"Yes, you may," Mendanbar said. "Willin, this is Kazul, the King of the Dragons, and she's very hungry. See if you can scare up something in the kitchen that would do for a dragon-sized meal."

"At once, Your Majesty," Willin said, bowing. "And may I congratulate you and your companions on your great achievement and welcome King Kazul to the Enchanted Forest."

"The welcome I'm interested in is dinner," Kazul said with a smile that showed all her teeth.

Willin backed away hastily. "Of course, of course. I'll see about it immediately."

"I'd better come with you," said Cimorene. "I've been Kazul's Chief Cook for over a year, and I know what she likes."

The two of them left, heading for the other side of the castle, with Kazul trailing hopefully behind them.

Mendanbar wasn't sure whether to be disappointed or relieved. He wanted very much to talk to Cimorene, but he wasn't sure how to tell her what he wanted to say, and anyway they certainly couldn't discuss the things he wanted to talk about with all these other people around.

"Mendanbar, have you got somewhere I could work on these without being disturbed?" Telemain asked, nodding at the load of wizards' staffs he was carrying.

"I wouldn't mind examining them myself," Morwen said.

"The blue room would be best, I think," Mendanbar said. "The light is better in my study, but there's a gargoyle in the corner who can be, um, difficult."

"We'll take the study," Morwen said decisively. "Light is important, and once Telemain gets involved, he won't notice any distractions."

"What about you?" Telemain asked, nettled.

Morwen sniffed. "I can handle considerably more than a mere gargoyle."

"All right," Mendanbar said. "As long as you're sure."

He showed them to the study and helped them get settled, then went down to the kitchen to see how Cimorene and Kazul were doing. He found Kazul in the rear courtyard, eating an enormous kettle of stew that had been intended to be supper for the entire castle. Cimorene was in the kitchen, her arms covered in flour to the elbows, rolling out pie crust and giving orders to the cook. Mendanbar stayed long enough to make sure that the cook would do whatever Cimorene told him to, and then Cimorene chased him away, saying that it was difficult enough to cook in a strange kitchen without people hovering over her.

"You don't have to cook anything," Mendanbar told her.

"I do if we want any dinner," Cimorene retorted. "Kazul is already eating everything that was ready for tonight, and she's going to want more as soon as she's finished. Your people aren't really prepared to cope with a visiting dragon."

"We've never had one before."

"Well, you have one now." Cimorene glanced toward the courtyard and lowered her voice. "I think we'll be staying for a few days at least, if that won't cause too many problems. Kazul needs to get her strength back before she tries to fly back to the Mountains of Morning."

"You can stay as long as you like," Mendanbar assured her. "Is there anything I can do to help?"

"You can let me get back to making dinner!" Cimorene said. She was smiling, but she obviously meant what she had said.

"All right. Call me if you need anything." Mendanbar bowed and left, feeling a little put out.

He went to the castle library, since his study was occupied, and poked about in the scrolls for a few minutes. Then he decided to check on Prince Rupert and his nephew. He found the middle-aged prince quickly enough, but he had to send someone to retrieve the young Crown Prince from the dungeon.

"Did you enjoy your stay?" Mendanbar asked when Crown Prince Jorillam arrived at last.

"It was all right," Jorillam said. He looked rumpled and vaguely dissatisfied. "But there weren't any rats. I thought there'd be rats. There wasn't a rack, either."

"Jorillam!" Prince Rupert said sharply. "It's not polite to complain about things like that. Where are your manners?"

"I don't understand," Jorillam said, frowning. "If there *were* rats and a rack, I'd be expected to object, wouldn't I? So why can't I complain when they *aren't* there?"

"It's not the same thing," Rupert told him. "I'm sorry, Your Majesty," he went on, turning to Mendanbar. "He's used to getting his own way. I'm afraid I haven't done a very good job of teaching him how to behave."

"I behave just fine," Jorillam said.

"I am beginning to understand why you wanted to abandon him in the Enchanted Forest," Mendanbar said to Prince Rupert.

Rupert flushed. "No, no, it's not that. I'm really

very fond of the boy. But I have an obligation, you know, and there's no getting out of it."

"You can leave me here, Uncle," Jorillam said persuasively. "That's abandoning me in the Enchanted Forest, isn't it?"

"I don't think so," Mendanbar put in quickly. He didn't want to think about the problems the young Crown Prince could cause if he stayed at the castle. "There are too many people here for it to count as abandonment."

Prince Rupert nodded gloomily. "I'm afraid you're right. And frankly, I'm not at all sure that abandoning him is the right notion. I just can't think of anything else wicked to do on short notice."

"But you *promised* you'd abandon me in the Enchanted Forest," Jorillam protested. "And I *want* to be abandoned and have all sorts of adventures and come home covered in glory."

"You're a little young for that," Mendanbar commented, studying the Crown Prince. He smiled suddenly as an idea came to him. "What you need is some proper training."

"There isn't time," Jorillam said smugly. "Uncle has to do something wicked to me right away."

"Ah, but that's just the point," Mendanbar said. He turned to Prince Rupert, ignoring Jorillam's suddenly wary expression. "Abandoning Crown Prince Jorillam won't do you any good, because he *wants* to be abandoned. Letting him have his own way isn't terribly wicked, even if it isn't good for him."

"I'm afraid you're right," Rupert said sadly.

"But Uncle—"

"On the other hand," Mendanbar went on, disregarding Jorillam's interjection, "if you promised you'd abandon him, breaking that promise would certainly be wicked. And if you sent him off to a private school for princes—"

"I don't want to go to school!"

"Oh, my." Prince Rupert looked from Mendanbar to Jorillam—who now looked thoroughly alarmed—and back. "I think I see what you're getting at. If he hates the idea, then it probably is wicked, even if it's good for him. And there's breaking the promise, too."

"And you wouldn't have to tell anyone at home what you'd done with him," Mendanbar said. "You could rule the country just as if you really had abandoned him in the forest, and no one would know. Surely misleading all those people would be wicked enough for your society."

"I think you're right," Prince Rupert said, smiling for the first time since Mendanbar had met him. "I really think you're right." His face fell suddenly. "But how am I going to find a good school before sunset tomorrow?"

"Don't worry about that," Mendanbar said reassuringly. "I know just the place. It's up in the Mountains of Morning, where no one is likely to run across it, and it's run by a dwarf named Herman. If you like, I'll send a messenger off right away to arrange things."

"No!" said Jorillam.

"That would be wonderful," said Prince Rupert with relief. "Ah, I don't suppose this Herman person would be willing to write a letter to the Society explaining matters?"

"I don't see why not," Mendanbar said. "But what do you want it for?"

"Just to confirm that I'm fulfilling the requirements," Prince Rupert explained. "It *is* a rather unusual arrangement, you see, and I want to be sure the Society will think I've been wicked enough."

"I understand," Mendanbar told him. "Don't worry about it. If Herman won't write you a negative enough letter, I'll send one myself. I'll bet even the Right Honorable Wicked Stepmothers' Traveling, Drinking, and Debating Society will believe the King of the Enchanted Forest."

18

*In Which Willin Finally Gets
to Arrange a Formal Celebration*

*F*or the next several days, Mendanbar was busier than
he could remember being in a long, long time. Besides
arranging for Crown Prince Jorillam's schooling, a
stream of messengers had to be sent to the dragons in
the Mountains of Morning to explain where their King
was and to warn them about the wizards.

Morwen and Telemain argued constantly about
what they were finding out from the wizards' staffs,
and when they weren't arguing, they were asking for
obscure reference books and peculiar ingredients for
their spells. Between the two of them, they kept the
small castle staff busy hunting for things.

The wizards themselves seemed to have disappeared completely, but Mendanbar didn't trust them

to stay gone. He spent several hours every day checking the entire network of magic that enveloped the Enchanted Forest, looking for the tangles that wizards with staffs always caused, so that he would know if any of them returned. In the process, he found several more burned-out areas where the wizards had stolen the magic of the forest. Fortunately, none of the charred spots were very big, but repairing them was not an easy task, and Mendanbar worried constantly about what would happen if a wizard sneaked into the forest and soaked up a larger patch before he could be melted.

He confided this worry to Cimorene on the third day after Kazul's rescue.

"What you really need is a way to keep them from soaking up magic in the first place," said Cimorene. "Then it wouldn't matter if they sneaked in, because they wouldn't be able to do any real harm."

"They could still cause plenty of trouble," Mendanbar said. "But you're right, it would solve a lot of problems. Unfortunately, I can't think of a way to stop them."

"Well, of course you can't," Cimorene said. "You don't know enough about wizards and that ridiculous magic-absorbing spell of theirs. Why don't you ask Telemain?"

So Mendanbar went off to find Telemain, who was with Morwen, working on the last of the wizards' staffs. At first, Telemain was a little annoyed at being interrupted, but when Mendanbar explained his problem, however, the magician nodded.

"An automatic spell to reroute any magical power

should do the trick," Telemain said. "That way, anything they try to grab will just slide back where it belongs, and there will never be any new holes to fix."

Morwen looked at Telemain in mild surprise. "You're slipping," she said. "I actually understood that."

"Can you make up an automatic spell for me?" Mendanbar asked quickly, before Telemain could take offense.

"It shouldn't be a problem," Telemain said. "It'll need some sort of anchor, though, or you'll have to keep checking to see if it's still working. Any ideas?"

The three of them discussed it for a few minutes, and finally Morwen suggested tying the spell to the sword. This turned out to be an even better idea than it first appeared. Working through the sword, Mendanbar could manipulate the power of the Enchanted Forest directly, and with Telemain's help he made the new spell an integral part of the forest's magic.

"What does that mean?" Cimorene asked when he sought her out to tell her how well her idea had worked.

"It means that if any wizards come into the Enchanted Forest, their staffs won't absorb any magic, ever, for as long as they stay," Mendanbar explained. "I won't even have to check the spell very often, because it's tied to the sword. As long as the sword is anywhere in the forest, the wizards can't do a thing."

Cimorene frowned. "They could still use the spells they have stored in their staffs, couldn't they? And what if you have to leave the Enchanted Forest again?"

"I'll have to take a different magic sword, that's all," Mendanbar said. "I ought to do that anyway, because of the way that one sprays magic around outside the forest. It's not exactly inconspicuous."

"Very true," Cimorene said with a smile.

They were silent together for a moment. Then Cimorene shook her head. "Kazul will be ready to leave tomorrow. She thinks she's ready today, but I told her not to push."

"I— That's good," Mendanbar said. He hesitated, then said tentatively, "I suppose you'll be going with her?"

"What else would I be doing?" Cimorene asked. She sounded more curious than sarcastic.

Mendanbar took a deep breath. "You could stay here. At the castle, I mean. With me." This wasn't coming out at all the way he had wanted it to, but it was too late to stop now. He hurried on, "As Queen of the Enchanted Forest, if you think you would like that. I would."

"Would you, really?"

"Yes," Mendanbar said, looking down. "I love you, and—and—"

"And you should have said that to begin with," Cimorene interrupted, putting her arms around him. Mendanbar looked up, and the expression on her face made his heart begin to pound.

"Just to be sure I have this right," Cimorene went on with a blinding smile, "did you just ask me to marry you?"

"Yes," Mendanbar said. "At least, that's what I meant."

"Good. I will."

Mendanbar tried to find something to say, but he was too happy to think. He leaned forward two inches and kissed Cimorene, and discovered that he didn't need to say anything at all.

The first person they told was, of course, Kazul. Mendanbar was a little nervous about it, because from what he'd heard, dragons tended to get testy when their princesses ran off with someone, but Kazul didn't seem to mind at all.

"Good for you," she said to Mendanbar. "And congratulations to the pair of you." Her eyelids lowered halfway, and she looked at Cimorene. "I'd been wondering how much longer you were going to stay."

"I don't know what you mean," Cimorene said indignantly. "I wasn't *planning* to leave! This just sort of happened."

"I know," Kazul said. "But you'd have gone soon in any case. Now that you've gotten things organized, there isn't really enough work to keep you busy in the Mountains of Morning. You wouldn't have stayed long, once you started to get bored."

"Living with dragons doesn't sound boring to me," Mendanbar said.

"That's because you've never done it," Kazul replied. "Being Queen of the Enchanted Forest will give Cimorene more scope for her talents."

"Then you really don't object?" Mendanbar asked.

"Why should I?" Kazul said. "You're a nice enough person, as humans go, and you've been very polite about the whole thing. That doesn't happen often. Normally, knights and princes just grab a princess and run. And most of the princesses don't even bother to say good-bye, much less give proper notice." She looked at Cimorene and sighed. "I'll miss your cooking, though."

"I can come back for a week or two, if you'd like, and train a replacement," Cimorene offered.

"I may take you up on that, once I find one," Kazul said thoughtfully.

"And in the meantime, you can come over for dinner a lot," Mendanbar said, and both Cimorene and Kazul smiled at him.

When Willin heard about the engagement, he was delighted. The wedding of the King of the Enchanted Forest was just the sort of vast formal occasion the elf had been craving, and he threw himself into the preparations with enthusiasm. He didn't even object when he learned that the bride wanted the King of the Dragons for her matron-of-honor and a witch for her bridesmaid.

"Kazul and Morwen are my best friends," Cimorene explained. "Besides, if I have them, Mother won't insist that my sisters be bridesmaids."

"You have sisters?" Mendanbar asked, somewhat taken aback.

Cimorene nodded. "Six of them. They're all perfectly lovely and sweet, and the sight of Kazul will probably scare them silly."

"Typical princesses," Mendanbar muttered, but without any active dislike. He didn't seem to mind foolish princesses much anymore, as long as he didn't have to marry one. It was amazing what a difference being engaged to Cimorene made.

"They aren't as featherbrained as they sound," Cimorene told him. "They just act as if they are."

"I don't think I like the sound of that," Mendanbar said. "Are you sure they won't want to be bridesmaids anyway? Maybe we should just elope."

"No, it's too late for that," Cimorene told him. "Don't worry about it, though. It will work out fine."

"If you say so," Mendanbar said, but he was not really convinced.

The note Cimorene's mother sent to acknowledge the engagement only increased Mendanbar's misgivings. *I am delighted to hear that you are going to be properly settled at last, Cimorene dear,* ran the note. *I am enclosing a list of relatives and family friends who ought certainly to be included in your wedding plans, however unconventional those may be. Your father wishes to know which half of the kingdom your betrothed would prefer, as he is anxious to get the paperwork out of the way as soon as possible.*

"Half the kingdom?" Mendanbar asked cautiously.

Cimorene looked more than a little put out. "It's the usual reward for rescuing a princess from a dragon. I hoped they'd forgotten about it, but I should have known better. Mother would never do anything so incorrect."

"Well, I don't want it. One kingdom is more than enough for me."

"Then you'd better write them immediately and tell them so," Cimorene advised. "Otherwise they'll have all the forms and documents and records written out, signed by twenty noble witnesses, and sealed by every member of Father's Council, and you'll never be able to get rid of it."

"I'll see to it at once."

"Good." Cimorene picked up the long list of names that had been enclosed with the note. "I'll take this in to Willin, so someone can start addressing the invitations."

"Do we *have* to invite all of them?"

"We might as well," Cimorene said. "We're asking everyone else. And most of them are family."

"I think it would be easier to elope," Mendanbar said.

The guest list was enormous. Almost all the dragons were coming, and so were a great many of their princesses, past and present. After some initial misgivings, Cimorene's entire family decided to attend, including all six of her sisters and their husbands, her fourteen nieces and nephews, her parents, three of her aunts, two uncles, seventeen cousins, and her fairy godmother. Queen Alexandra was also coming, along with all twelve of her daughters. Mendanbar couldn't help feeling a little nervous about that, out of habit. All the kings and queens and princes and grand dukes who lived around the edges of the Enchanted Forest had had to be invited, and so had most of the odd and unusual people who lived inside the forest itself. Even the ogres and trolls had agreed to behave themselves if they were allowed to be present. In fact, the only people who *hadn't* been invited were the wizards.

"This wedding will be the best and most prestigious event in years!" Willin said happily as the acceptances poured in.

"It's certainly going to be the biggest," Mendanbar said, gazing at the stacks of paper in mild amazement. "Where are we going to *put* them all?"

"You are not to worry about that, Your Majesty," Willin told him sternly. "It is *my* job to oversee the preparations, and that includes arranging an appropriate place to hold the ceremony and the reception afterward."

"I really think it would have been easier to elope," Mendanbar grumbled.

In the end, they decided to hold the wedding in Fire-Flower Meadow. The gargoyle in Mendanbar's study complained about the decision long and loudly, because it would obviously be unable to attend, but the meadow was the only open area in the entire Enchanted Forest that would be large enough for the enormous crowd of guests.

"I bet you think that makes it all right," the gargoyle told Mendanbar and Cimorene several days before the wedding. "Just because *you* want to have hundreds and hundreds of people at *your* wedding, *I'm* supposed to smile and say I don't mind being left out. Well, it isn't all right and I won't do it!"

"I wouldn't expect you to smile about anything," Mendanbar muttered.

Cimorene studied the gargoyle thoughtfully. "If you're that eager to come, I suppose we could take the molding in that corner apart and find someone to bring you down to the field to watch," she offered.

The gargoyle looked down at her in alarm. "Take me *apart*? Oh, no, you don't! I'm not stupid. I know what would happen. Even if you managed to get me out of here without damaging me, you'd forget to put me back afterward, and I'd spend centuries in a storeroom somewhere. Dust and dry rot!"

"Well, then I'm afraid all I can do is stop in before I leave for the ceremony," Cimorene said. "Unless Telemain can fix up a spell on one of the windows so you can watch from here."

"I don't want that magician messing around with anything in my—wait a minute, did you say you'd stop in? You mean, here? In this room?"

"That's what she said," Mendanbar told it.

"I wasn't talking to you," the gargoyle said. Looking back at Cimorene, it went on, "You mean, you'd come and see me *before* the wedding?"

"That's right," Cimorene said, nodding.

"*Right* before? All dressed up and everything?"

"Of course," Cimorene promised.

"Hot dog!" said the gargoyle. "I'll take it! Oh, boy, I can hardly wait! This is going to be even better than going to the wedding."

"It is?" Mendanbar said suspiciously. "Why?"

"Because *I'll* get to see her all dolled up before *you* do, that's why," the gargoyle answered smugly. "Everybody knows the groom doesn't get to see the bride on the wedding day until the ceremony. And she's going to stop in here first! Oh, boy, oh, boy!"

Mendanbar looked at Cimorene.

"He's right, you know," Cimorene said apologetically. "And I've promised."

"He's never going to let me forget this," Mendanbar muttered and left to talk to Telemain about setting up Fire-Flower Meadow for the wedding.

Despite Willin's determination to handle the wedding plans himself, there were a number of things only Mendanbar could do. Among the most important was making sure that Fire-Flower Meadow and the area around it stayed firmly in one spot on the day of the wedding, so that all the guests could find it. This was not an easy thing to arrange. Even with Telemain's help, it took Mendanbar several days' worth of work before he was positive no one would miss the wedding because of a shift in the forest.

The night before the ceremony, Mendanbar and Telemain went over the whole field an inch at a time, to make certain that all the fire-flowers had been picked (so that none of the guests would get an accidental hotfoot) and to take care of any lingering minor enchantments. They found two princesses who had been turned into pinks, a frog prince, and a hedgehog that had once been somebody's groom. All of them were grateful to be disenchanted and very happy to be invited to the wedding.

The day of the wedding dawned bright and clear. Telemain had spent most of the previous week making sure that it would, while explaining to anyone who would listen that weather magic worked best if one set it up over a long period of time, which was what made it so difficult. The guests started arriving early, and Mendanbar was kept busy greeting them.

A large corner of the field had been roped off as a landing place for dragons, and for most of the morning the sky was full of flashing green wings. Ballimore and Dobbilan—who had come the previous evening to make sure their Cauldron of Plenty would have enough time to produce a proper wedding dinner for so many guests—directed traffic, as they were the only ones large enough for the dragons to see clearly from a distance amid the growing crowd.

Jack was early, too. He parked his wagon in a corner of the field and did a brisk business selling seven-league boots, cloaks of invisibility, and magic rings (along with wrapping paper and tape) to those who had forgotten to bring wedding presents. Nearby, all nine of Morwen's cats prowled on, around, under, and through the stacks of gifts that covered the six long benches that had been set out to hold them. Whenever someone brought a new package to lay on the benches, three of the cats would converge on him and purr loudly, while the others kept a watchful eye on the rest of the presents.

Slowly, the meadow filled up. Everyone was in a good mood, everyone was on his or her best behavior, and everyone was trying to be helpful. Even Cimorene's family seemed to be having a good time. Her father was deep in conversation with Dobbilan, discussing ways of discouraging marauding giants. Several of her sisters were comparing notes with the dragons' ex-princesses, while her mother helped Queen Alexandra and her daughters (who did not seem nearly as awful as Mendanbar remembered) set bowls of punch and trays of sandwiches on a table at the far end of the meadow for people to nibble on until dinner was served.

Herman and his flock of children—including Crown Prince Jorillam—arrived and bought several bags of walnuts from Jack to feed the squirrels. Jorillam was delighted to discover that the squirrels would give him advice about quests. He went through three bags of nuts before the ceremony began and had to be almost dragged to his seat when the time came. His uncle, Prince Rupert, showed up at the last minute, wearing a black cloak and an enormous fake mustache. He looked very wicked and thoroughly pleased with himself.

Finally, everyone was there, everything was ready, and it was time. Resplendent in deep green velvet, milk white satin, and his best crown, Mendanbar waited nervously while the musicians, a talented group of Goldwing-Shadowmusic elves, began the wedding march. Willin, who had at first argued—but not very hard—that he was not a proper person to be a grooms-man because he was Mendanbar's steward, came down the long, open aisle with Morwen, who was wearing her best black robe. Following them came Kazul, the matron-of-honor, and Telemain, Mendanbar's best man. Then came Cimorene, and Mendanbar forgot about everyone else.

Instead of her usual crown of black braids, Cimorene had let her hair hang in loose, shining waves down her back. She wore a wreath of fire-flowers, specially enchanted to burn without being hot or setting anything ablaze; from the wreath hung a veil of silver lace. Her bouquet was of fire-flowers, too, and her dress shimmering snow-silk trimmed with silver. She was stunningly beautiful.

The ceremony went by in a blur, but Mendanbar was pretty sure he hadn't made any mistakes because suddenly he was kissing Cimorene and everyone was cheering. He felt like cheering himself, except he would have had to stop kissing Cimorene.

A finger poked him surreptitiously. With considerable reluctance, Mendanbar broke away from Cimorene and turned.

"Enough," Telemain said in a voice so low Mendanbar could hardly hear it over the cheering. "Now it's time for the party."

Mendanbar looked at Cimorene, who gave him a wry smile as if to say that she didn't think it was enough, either, but there was nothing they could do about it now. He looked back at Telemain.

"I *knew* we should have eloped," he said.

Cimorene laughed and shook her head at him. "You don't really mean that, any more than you mean it when you complain about the gargoyle," she said, taking his arm.

"Who told you that?"

"The gargoyle did," she admitted, and they both laughed. "Come enjoy the party."

Arm in arm, the King and Queen of the Enchanted Forest went to accept the congratulations of their guests.

Cimorene, Mendanbar, and Kazul's adventures
continue in...

Calling on Dragons

The third book in the Enchanted Forest Chronicles

Turn the page for a hilarious sneak peak!

1

In Which a Great Many Cats
Express Opinions

Deep in the Enchanted Forest, in a neat gray house with a wide porch and a red roof, lived the witch Morwen and her nine cats. The cats were named Murgatroyd, Fiddlesticks, Miss Eliza Tudor, Scorn, Jasmire, Trouble, Jasper Darlington Higgins IV, Chaos, and Aunt Ophelia, and not one of them looked anything like a witch's cat. They were tabby, gray, white, tortoiseshell, ginger, seal brown, and every other cat color in the world except a proper and witchy black.

Morwen didn't look like a witch any more than her cats looked as if they should belong to one. For one thing, she was much too young—less than thirty —and she had neither wrinkles nor warts. In fact, if she hadn't been a witch people might have said she was quite pretty. Her hair was the same ginger color as Jasmine's fur, and she had hazel eyes and a delicate, pointed chin. Because she was very short, she had to stand quite straight (instead of hunching over in correct witch fashion) if she wanted people to pay attention to her. And she was nearsighted, so she always had to wear glasses; hers had rectangular lenses. She refused even to put on the tall, pointed hats most witches wore, and she dressed in loose black robes because they were comfortable and practical, not because they were traditional.

All of this occasionally annoyed people who cared more about the propriety of her dress than the quality of her spells.

"You ought to turn him into a toad," Trouble said, looking up from washing his right front paw. Trouble was a large, lean gray tomcat with a crooked tail and a recently acquired ragged ear. He had never told Morwen exactly how he had damaged either the tail or the ear, but from the way he acted she assumed he had won a fight with something.

"Who should I turn into a toad?" Morwen asked, looking an unusually long way down. She was sitting sideways on her broomstick, floating comfortably next to the top of the front door, with a can of gold paint in one hand and a small paintbrush in the other. Above the door, in black letters partly edged in gold, ran the message "NONE OF THIS NONSENSE, PLEASE," which Morwen was engaged in repainting.

"That fellow who's making all the fuss about pointy hats and respect for tradition," Trouble replied. "The one you were grumbling about a minute ago—what's his name?"

"Arona Michaelear Grinogion Vamist," Morwen

recited, putting the final gold line along the bottom of the "L" in "PLEASE." "And it's a tempting thought. But someone worse would probably replace him."

"Turn them all into toads. I'll help."

"Toads?" purred a new voice. A small ginger cat slithered out the open window and arched her back, then stretched out along the window ledge, where she could watch the entire front yard without turning her head. "I'm tired of toads. Why don't you turn somebody into a mouse for a change?" The ginger cat ran her tongue around her lips.

"Good morning, Jasmine," Morwen said. "I'm not planning to turn anyone into anything, at the moment, but I'll keep it in mind."

"That means she won't do it," said Trouble. He looked at his right paw, decided it was clean enough for the time being, and began washing his left.

"Won't do what?" said Fiddlesticks, poking his brown head out of the front door. "Who's not doing it? Why shouldn't he—or is that she? And who says so?"

"Turn someone into a mouse; Morwen; I certainly don't see why not; and she does," Jasmine said in a bored tone, and pointedly turned her head away.

"Mice are nice." Fiddlesticks shouldered the door open another inch and trotted out onto the porch. "So are fish. I haven't had any fish in a long time." He paused underneath Morwen's broom and looked up expectantly.

"You had fish for dinner yesterday," Morwen said without looking down. "And you ate enough breakfast this morning to satisfy three ordinary cats, so don't try to pretend you're starving. It won't work."

"Someone's coming," Jasmine observed from the window.

Trouble stood up and ambled to the edge of the porch. "It's the Chairwitch of the Deadly Nightshade Gardening Club. Wasn't she just here last week?"

"It's Archaniz? Oh, bother," said Morwen, sticking her paintbrush into the can. "Has she got that idiot cat Grendel with her? I told her not to bring him anymore, but nine times out of ten she doesn't listen."

Fiddlesticks joined Trouble at the top of the porch steps. "I don't see him. I don't see anyone but her. I don't want to see her, either. She doesn't like me."

"That's because you talk too much," Trouble told him.

"I'm going inside," Fiddlesticks announced. "Then I won't have to see her. Maybe someone's dropped some fish on the floor," he added hopefully as he trotted into the house.

Morwen landed her broomstick and stood up, just as the Chairwitch reached the porch steps. The Chairwitch looked exactly as a witch ought: tall, with a crooked black hat, stringy black hair, sharp black eyes, a long, bony nose, and a wide, thin-lipped mouth. She hunched over as she walked, leaning on her broom as if it were a cane.

Morwen put the paint can on the window ledge next to Jasmine, set her broom against the wall, and said, "Good morning, Archaniz."

"Good morning, Morwen," Chairwitch Archaniz croaked. "What's this I hear about you growing lilacs in your garden?"

"Since I don't know what you've heard, I can't

answer you," Morwen replied. "Come in and have some cider."

Archaniz pounded the end of her broom against the porch floor, breaking some of the twigs and scattering bits of dust and bark in all directions. "Don't be provoking, Morwen. You're a witch. You're supposed to grow poison oak and snakeroot and wolfsbane, not lilacs. You'll get thrown out of the Deadly Nightshade Gardening Club if you aren't careful."

"Nonsense. Where in the rules does it say that I can't grow what I please in my own garden?"

"It doesn't," Archaniz admitted. "And I'll tell you right away that you aren't the only one who puts a few lilacs and daylilies in with the rampion and henbane. Why, I've got a perfectly ordinary patch of daisies in the corner myself."

"Daisies." Jasmine snorted softly. "She would."

"But I've been getting complaints," Archaniz continued, "and I have to do *something* about them."

"What sort of complaints?"

"That the Deadly Nightshade Gardening Club is too normal for witches," Archaniz said gloomily. "That all we grow are everyday plants like cabbages and apples—"

"Apples are a basic necessity for witches," Morwen said. "And everyday plants don't turn the people who eat them into donkeys. Who's complaining?"

"Some fellow with an impossible name—Arona Mc-something-or-other."

"Arona Michaelear Grinogion Vamist?"

The Chairwitch nodded. "That's the one. I've gotten six regular letters and two by Eagle Express in the past month. He says he's going to write a letter to the *Times* next."

"He would," Trouble muttered. "I *said* you should turn him into a toad."

"That idea sounds better all the time," Morwen told Trouble. Then she looked back at Archaniz, who of course had not understood a word Trouble had said. "Vamist isn't a witch," Morwen said. "He's an idiot. Why worry about what he says?"

"That's all very well, Morwen, but if he convinces people he's right, it'll ruin our image. And if people think we're not dangerous, they'll come around asking for love potions and penny curses whenever they like. We'll be so busy mixing up cures for gout that we won't have time for the things *we* want to do. Look what happened to the sorceresses!"

"I haven't seen many of them around lately."

Archaniz nodded. "They got a reputation for being kind and beneficent, and the next thing you knew everyone was begging them for help. Most of them moved to remote islands or deep forests, just to get away from the pestering. It's all very well for you, Morwen, living out here in the Enchanted Forest anyway, but I—"

A loud yowl interrupted the Chairwitch in mid-sentence. An instant later, four cats tore around the corner of the house. The one in front was a heavy, short-legged tomcat with yellow eyes and fur as black as night. Behind him came a fat, long-haired tabby tomcat and two females, one a large calico and the other a fluffy white cat with blue eyes. The black cat streaked out into the front yard, made a hairpin turn, and leapt for the porch, where he clawed his way up Archaniz's skirts to a perch on her shoulder.

The three pursuing cats jumped gracefully onto the porch railing and sat down, curling their tails around their feet, just as Fiddlesticks poked his head out of the front door.

"What's all the noise about? Who's shouting? Is it a fight? Who's winning? Can I join?" With every question, Fiddlesticks pushed a little farther, until he was entirely outside the house, staring up at Archaniz and the cat on her shoulder. "Who's *that*?"

"Mrow!" said the black cat in a complaining tone. "Yow wow mrrrum!"

"Oh, yeah?" said Trouble. "Well, *your* father wears *boots!*"

Morwen gave the black cat a speculative look. "One of these days, I am going to have to work up a spell that will let me understand other people's cats as well as my own," she said to Archaniz. "What was that about?"

"We caught him nosing around in back of the garden," the long-haired tabby growled.

"He had no business there," the white cat added primly. "He's not one of *us*, after all. So we thought we would drive him away."

"Stupid creature was babbling something about a rabbit," the calico cat said with a disdainful look at the black cat. "As if that was any excuse."

"Why didn't you call me?" Trouble demanded. "I never get to have any fun." Radiating hurt pride, he stalked to the far end of the porch and disappeared into a large clump of beebalm.

"You know, people have been trying to perfect a universal cat-translating spell for years," Archaniz said to Morwen in a dry tone. She glanced at the cats on the porch railing. "If you *do* come up with one, I'd like a copy for myself."

"Nosy old biddy," said the calico cat.

"On second thought, perhaps it would be better if I left things as they are," Morwen said.

"Being disagreeable, are they?" Archaniz said knowingly. "It's only to be expected. Who ever heard of a polite cat?"

The black cat hissed. "Grendel!" said Archaniz. "Behave yourself. It wasn't that bad, and besides, you can use the exercise."

"He certainly can," said the calico cat.

"What's all this racket?" rumbled a low, sleepy cat voice from under the porch. "Dash it, can't a fellow take a nap in peace?" A moment later, a long cream-and-silver cat oozed around the steps to blink at the growing assembly above him.

"That's another thing, Morwen," Archaniz said, scowling at the newcomer. "Cats and witches go together, I admit. And I know they're a big help with your spells, but one really ought to observe some reasonable limits."

"I do," said Morwen. All nine cats were useful, particularly when it came to working long, involved spells that required both concentration and power. Nine cats working together could channel a lot of magic. To explain all this would sound uncomfortably like bragging, however, so Morwen only added, "Anyway, I like cats."

"She is simply jealous because we're all smarter than *he* is," the white cat informed Morwen with a look at the black cat on Archaniz's shoulder.

"What, all of you?" Morwen said, raising an eyebrow.

"All of us," the white cat said firmly. "Even Fiddlesticks."

"I'm very smart," Fiddlesticks agreed. "I'm *lots* smarter than Fatso there. Don't you think I'm smart, Morwen?"

Grendel hissed and bunched together as if he were preparing to launch himself from Archaniz's shoulder. Hastily, Archaniz put up her free hand to hold him back. "Perhaps I had better leave now," she said. "We can finish our discussion some other—"

"There's a big garden show coming up in Lower Sandis," Morwen said thoughtfully. "Why doesn't the Deadly Nightshade Garden Club enter an exhibit? If we all work together, we should be able to put together something quite impressive."

Archaniz considered. "Monkshood and snakeroot and so on? In a large black tent."

"And if everyone sends one or two really exotic things—"

"Morwen, you're a genius! People will talk about it for years, and that Airy McAiling Grinny person won't have a leg to stand on."

"I don't think it will be that simple," Morwen cautioned. "But an exhibit will buy us time to find out why he's so interested in making witches do things *his* way. And stop him."

"Of course," the Chairwitch said happily. "Let's

see—Kanikak grows Midnight fire-flowers, and I have half a dozen Giant Weaselweeds. If I can talk Wully into letting us use her smokeblossoms . . ."

"I'll contribute two Black Diamond snake lilies and an invisible dusk-blooming chokevine," Morwen said. "I won't keep you any longer now; just let me know when you've got things arranged. Chaos, Miss Eliza, Scorn, wait for me inside, if you please."

The three cats sitting on the railing looked at each other. Then Chaos, the long-haired tabby, jumped down and sauntered past Fiddlesticks into the house. The white cat, Miss Eliza Tudor, followed, tail high, and Fiddlesticks fell in behind her, apparently without even thinking about what he was doing. Scorn sat where she was, staring stubbornly at Morwen.

"I'm not leaving while that idiot of hers is still here," Scorn said with a sidelong glance at Grendel and Archaniz. "There's no telling *what* he might get up to."

As this did not seem unreasonable, for a cat, Morwen let it pass. She walked Archaniz out into the yard, where there was plenty of room for a takeoff, and bade her a polite good-bye. As soon as the Chairwitch was out of sight above the trees, Morwen turned to go back inside. Jasper Darlington Higgins IV was sitting in front of the porch steps, watching her.

"Was that a good idea?" he said. "Invisible dusk-blooming chokevines aren't exactly easy to find, you know. Much less to grow. And you haven't got any, unless you've added them to the garden since early this morning."

"I'm well aware of that," Morwen said. "But I've been wanting some for a long time, to put along the fence by the back gate. Now I've got a good excuse to hunt them up."

"As long as you know what you're getting into," Jasper said. "Can I go back to sleep now, or is there going to be more noisy excitement?"

"Go to sleep," said Morwen. As she climbed the porch steps, she gave Scorn a pointed glare. Dignity dripping from every whisker, Scorn jumped down from the railing and walked into the house. Morwen shook her head, picked up her broomstick and her paint can, and followed.